An Officer and a Gentleman Wanted

Beverley Watts

BaR Publishing

This book is dedicated to all the wonderful International Officer Cadets who made my time at Dartmouth so memorable...

Contents

Author's Note

Britannia Royal Naval College (or BRNC as it's known in naval circles) is the British Royal Navy's officer training establishment. It's a magnificently imposing Edwardian building built high on a hill overlooking the small yachting haven of Dartmouth in the south west of England. The location was chosen for the safe sheltered harbour provided by the River Dart (and possibly for the difficulty that cadets would have getting to the bright lights of... well anywhere).

It is an accepted fact that the Royal Navy's officer training standards are among the best in the world and consequently a number of foreign navies who don't have their own training establishments send their young officers to be trained by the RN.

Many of the International officer cadets who come through Dartmouth are from the Middle East and require English Language Training to enable them to undertake the Royal Navy's Officer Training Course which is obviously delivered in English.

During my time at the College, I worked for a private training company whose job was to provide English

Language Training to the International Cadets thus enabling them to complete their officer training alongside the British Cadets.

I can tell you hand on heart that in 8 years there was never a dull moment...

Lastly, please note that this book is a purely fictional romantic comedy (very) loosely based on my wonderful experiences while I was at BRNC...

I hope that you enjoy reading the book as much as I enjoyed writing it.

Week 1

Monday 7 September

New term. New Intake. New OFFICERS…

I wonder if he's arrived yet. Maria, my clairvoyant told me in no uncertain terms that I was finally going to meet Mr Right this year.

We're going to be friends first. (No shagging on the first date…)

He's going to stimulate me mentally. (Does that mean no shagging at all?)

Bugger – she never said how long we have to be friends for first…

My internal ramblings are cut short by the car ferry's arrival in Dartmouth – probably a blessing really. I don't want to be reminded of exactly how long it's been since my last carnal adventure – wasn't really an adventure at all actually; there's a lot of truth in the saying that 'officers have more mouth than trousers'.

Still, I promised myself when I started working at Britannia Royal Naval College – the Royal Navy's premier training establishment – that I would eventually become that most envied of creatures – an officer's wife.

I might be divorced and in my mid 40s, but it doesn't mean I've given up on romance – I've seen An Officer and a Gentleman…

0800 There is always a first day back queue at the College gate.

Bloody hell, do the guards want to know what EVERYONE did during their leave period? Some of us (namely civvies) don't actually get leave periods, we're permanent fixtures – never leaving the site except to go home and do the washing.

Damn, I'm going to be late – Oh I forgot, I've been promoted now so it doesn't matter if I'm late.

'Head of English Language Training' has a great ring to it – It's even written on my badge and my security pass – how cool is that?

MS BEVERLEY WILKINS
HEAD OF ENGLISH LANGUAGE TRAINING

This is the beginning of my meteoric rise to the very highest echelons of the company; I am certain of it – my time has come...

0810 I finally get through the gate in to the College grounds after waving my ID at the guard and drive slowly up the winding road with the beautiful red brick building of the Naval College towering above me on the left and the breathtaking view of the River Dart below me on the other. I park the car in my new 'Head of English Language' parking space which is great because it's not 3 miles from the College entrance like the last one (murder on the feet in high heels). Still, I'll probably miss that little gambol first thing in the morning being dragged along by my dog Nelson (after the Admiral of course, not the politician) desperate for his first wee...

Actually, delete that – no I won't miss it at all.

I haven't brought Nelson in today – thought I'd try for a bit of authority and respect from the teachers before they completely ignore me and focus on their favourite Irish terrier.

Ok, I walk into the main College building through the back entrance and I'm standing at the beginning of the longest and most lethal corridor in existence.

'The Corridor' has brought the very greatest to their knees – usually in the most humiliating circumstances with everybody and his dog watching. I think I might have the record for the only person working at the College who has not actually gone arse over tit on the polished floor.

Why don't they carpet the floor if it's so dangerous? *Because it's a listed building...*

What are a few broken arms and legs when compared to British history?

But that's ok because *I know how to do it* (and in heels). It's not the height of your shoes - believe me I've seen the best of them go down in flatties...

It's the soles on your shoes.

And the Royal Navy in all its wisdom actually makes its officers wear leather soles – quite funny really; it certainly makes them a little less pompous...

So here I am, just outside the College Chapel looking right down at least 100yards of hallowed corridor culminating at the Senior Gunroom Mess and I'm wearing new shoes.

Always makes me sweat a bit.

Experience tells me it pays to take it slowly; first of all slide left foot backwards and forwards in a tentative motion to gauge the 'grip' factor. Then, on to the right foot – backwards, forwards... Then cautiously take the first step and the second....

0820 I finally arrive at the English Language School halfway down The Corridor and up 2 flights of stairs. (Actually above the Commodore's office – not that I'm name dropping or anything.)

It's taken me nearly 10 minutes – there is a reason why I hold the College record despite wearing 3½ heels. Mind you, I'll get faster once I've worn the shoes in a bit.

I can't believe it – I now have my own office. I might as well be working for the Ministry Of Defence. All I need now is a sofa and a coffee table…

I wander along the Language School corridor and stick my head in each of the classrooms feeling very territorial.

I've got 10 minutes before the teachers start arriving. Just time for a quick coffee and a ginger nut.

1030 It feels like I've done a day's work – I'm already longing for the time when all I had to do was teach.
And the International Cadets aren't even due to arrive for another 2 days…

I also chaired my first staff meeting this morning.
Top on the agenda? Where was Nelson? Was he ill? Should we send him a get well bone?

I'm not always sure it's a good thing the College allows dogs to come to work.

It took me a while, but I finally managed to drag the conversation back to the matter at hand; namely how many International Young Officer Cadets we can expect for English Language Training this term…

8 Officer Cadets from the Kuwait Navy: Quite intelligent, lots of money, very friendly, reasonably motivated.

15 Officer Cadets from the Kuwait Coastguard: Not quite as intelligent, lots of money, very friendly, completely lazy.

10 Officer Cadets from the Qatar Coastguard: Ditto – with lots of rich relatives in London.

1 Officer Cadet from another Navy who shall not be named as he's a member of the country's royal family but we're not supposed to know…

All we have to do is make them ready and capable of completing the Royal Navy's Young Officer Course alongside the British Young Officers starting in January.

Just under 14 weeks.

No pressure...

I call a quick end to the meeting determined to get down to the Wardroom for Stand Easy. (I know, made me snigger when I first heard it too – it's amazing how quick you get used to these quaint naval terms though.)

That gives me half an hour to find out the latest gossip (dits in navy speak); check out the new officers just arrived and get reacquainted with those back from leave.

I take a slow stroll down The Corridor towards the Wardroom. Although this is actually the Officers' Mess, we're allowed in because we're classed as 'lecturers' – even though we're only civvies and actually work for a private company. This fact causes untold consternation and distress to older and more distinguished members of the Mess – lowers the tone don't you know. I happen to think that a lot of the officers manage to do that all on their own – without any help from the civilians in the College – that's why it's such fun to work here.

I make a quick stop at the heads (toilets to us mere mortals not in uniform; mixed of course – this is the Royal Navy) and on in to the Wardroom.

1100 Time to go back to work. I didn't get to see all the newbie officers, but a bit disappointing so far.

Met the College's new Training Executive Officer Sam (thought the title was Training *Execution* Officer when I first started working here – remember thinking at the time that it was a bit extreme...) He's quite cute in a cheeky kind of way – maybe a bit young for me. In fact he actually looked about 20. Still, apparently St Vincent Squadron has a new Senior Squadron Officer arriving this morning which sounds promising.

And of course the College has two squadrons, I haven't met Cunningham Squadron's senior officer yet so you never know... (Personally I love my optimism although it could possibly be misconstrued on odd occasions as reality denial.)

Ok, Head of English Language Training cap on for the next hour and a half followed by lunch and then the Commodore's address. - it never feels like the term's really started until after the Commodore's waxed lyrically about his plans for the coming term - and lastly, a meeting with Commander Naval Training and Education to discuss the upcoming International Cadets arriving this term.

Never let it be said that I don't mix with the crème de la crème.

1330 (24 hour clock – this *is* a military establishment.) I've just got time to visit the bathroom before heading up to the concert hall for the Commodore's address.

Lunch was very interesting – I ended up sitting next to said new St Vincent Squadron Officer – could it be a sign?

He had a really nice face – hair was pretty much completely grey (but at least he had some) so he must be fairly near my age.

Will reserve judgement for later...

1700 Just come out of a looong meeting with Commander Naval Training and Education.

Too knackered to pass further comment.

1710 Sitting in the ferry queue waiting to get across the River Dart and home to Paignton.

1720 Still sitting in the ferry queue.

1730 Still sitting in the ferry queue. (Believe me, road rage has nothing on ferry rage – thinking of starting a therapy group for those forced to confront queue jumpers…)

1805 Home finally. It's lovely living by the seaside but sometimes it takes so long to do the 7 miles from Dartmouth to Paignton that I think I'd be better to live on board alongside the cadets (another cute Naval colloquialism referring to the fact that the College is built like a ship.)

1810 Ah the relief, just kicked off my shoes and sitting down with the first glass of wine. I can tell that Nelson's glad to see me because he's enthusiastically licking my feet – quite nice actually…

Think I need to get out more.

Tuesday 8 September

1 020   I lift my head from answering the mountains of emails that being the boss seems to entail and decide I can now legitimately and with good conscience take a break.

But before I head down to the Wardroom, I check out the important bits – the new St Vincent (forgotten his name) Senior Squadron Officer might be there.
I stand in front of the full length mirror in my office and stare critically at my reflection.

5 feet nothing and 120 pounds; maybe a little overweight (although I prefer the term curvy) – definitely not Catherine Zeta Jones but not quite Bridget Jones either. The suit jacket's a bit tight but I don't do it up so that's ok. The 3½ heels make me look a bit taller.

Shoulder length blonde hair (ok so it's highlighted). My face is actually quite attractive, although it definitely looks better without my reading glasses on, not so many wrinkles – sorry, laughter lines. Brown eyes, generous lips – especially when vamped up with my favourite red lipstick which always makes me feel in control...

And the suit gives me that business edge – you know what? I really do look the part.

Then I glance over at Nelson who in time honoured tradition of his first day back is snoring on the easy chair in the corner of the office, flat on his back, legs in the air showing off all his glory in complete abandon. (He can just about fit in the chair if he squidges his head round to the side – he looks like Tramp from the Disney film but with ginger fur.)

Not really the image a go-getting business woman wants the world to see, but at the end of the day I don't care – I think he's irresistible - most of the time.

En route I meet up with Sarah – my partner in crime for all College activities taking place after 6pm (and some before...)

We walk together making sure we keep to the middle of The Corridor (more traffic, so not as polished) and discuss the new arrivals this term.

I ask her if she's been introduced to the new St Vincent Senior Squadron Officer and when she nods her head, I ask the dreaded question

"Is he married?"

Now this is a small point that doesn't seem to register with every naval officer. The 'out of sight, out of mind' ethos is taken to a whole new level in the Royal Navy.

Unfortunately Sarah isn't able to shed any light on the situation, but promises to investigate further and, as she runs the College Planning Department, she might be in a better position to ask without making herself look a complete tit.

Sadly the new VSO wasn't at Stand Easy – I can't keep saying 'The St Vincent Senior Squadron Officer'; it's such a mouthful and the Royal Navy does love its TLAs (Three Letter Abbreviations...)

Plus I can't actually remember his name, and now I'm beginning to forget what he looks like.

Is that a sign?

Oh well, maybe he'll be there at lunch time.

1530 I haven't managed to get any lunch, absolutely snowed under getting ready for the Internationals arriving tomorrow.

I haven't even had time to take Nelson out for a wee – he's looking at me very reproachfully with his legs in plaits.

Ignoring his plaintive looks, (he's got the bladder of a rhinoceros) I grab a coffee - this must be my 15th today, I'm definitely beginning to feel a bit twitchy - and head into the International Liaison Office (ILO) which is next to the language school.

To most International Officer Cadets, this is the most important room in the College. The staff here deal with everything from arranging travel visas to explaining why someone's 2nd cousin over from Abu Dhabi can't bunk down on his cabin floor for a couple of weeks...

The International Liaison Officer (ILO – why have 2 different TLAs when you can use the same one twice) John is on the phone, so I wait, patiently nursing my caffeine fix.

He's speaking with Rashid, the Military Attaché's personal assistant at the Qatar Embassy in London.
Turns out that only half the Qatari Coastguard will be arriving tomorrow – the rest haven't had chance to visit Harrods yet before venturing down to the wilds of Dartmouth.

"This is a military establishment." John's voice is getting louder – always a bad sign. "They can't just turn up when they damn well please."

Can't quite hear Rashid's response but John turning a darker shade of purple can't be a good sign.

"So how many have we got?" I butt in while John's still spluttering (he does tend to waffle a bit so I always take advantage of any gaps in the conversation – spluttering counts as a gap.)

"Four arriving tomorrow, the rest on Thursday."

"No problem, we'll just postpone the language tests until Friday."

I've learned not to get upset about the tardiness of some Arab nations. We once had a contingent of Qataris who were supposedly en route to the UK – they were 'in the air' for about 5 weeks in total...

"So that gives us 27 arriving tomorrow?"

"Supposedly."

Strategic retreat seems the best option.

1715 I love to take a last look around the classrooms when everyone's left; it's so peaceful.

I reflect on past International Cadets who have passed through our hands on the way to Military stardom – some of them not even 18 when they arrive and little more than petulant teenagers, (albeit petulant teenagers driving anything from a Mercedes to a Porsche...)

I stand at the classroom window and stare out over the Parade Ground into the late afternoon sunshine. Beyond, the College grounds slope away towards the River Dart and the sea.

To the right is the yachting haven of Dartmouth and to the left, the Dart snakes around towards the market town of Totnes. I can just see the aft end (see I know my aft from my forward) of HMS Hindustan, the training ship moored alongside the College at Sandquay.
Sometimes the beauty of this place simply takes my breath away.

1730 In the ferry queue.

1740 Still in the ferry queue.

1750 Still in the ferry queue – had to stop the guy 2 cars in front of me from conducting a lobotomy on a bewildered holiday maker who insisted he didn't know where the end of the queue was (they all say that.)

1800 Definitely on the next one if we can convince the ferry guys to refuse to allow said holiday maker 'aka most vile queue jumper' to reap the benefits of his heinous crime...

1830 Back at home and the kitchen looks like a scene out of World War 3. There's a note from my youngest daughter Frankie on the kitchen table:

'Will clean up when I get back'

Not knowing whether that's likely to be tonight or next year, I grab a glass of wine (medicinal) and set to.

1850 The kitchen, while not exactly sparkly, is no longer a breeding ground for penicillin. Frankie's the most wonderful cook – I just wish she'd do it somewhere else.

I grab a second glass of wine (I think it's the second) and head down to mum's flat on the floor below.

Ok so I live with my mother – well not exactly WITH, more on top of – but it works for us, and converting a large house in to 2 flats definitely gave us much more for our money.

What can I say? We have separate entrances and mum can't hear a thing without her hearing aid.

We moved here about 6 years ago after my 23 year marriage came to an abrupt end when my husband decided that I didn't need him anymore. Unfortunately he forgot to ask me first! Luckily our girls were 18 and 14 when he decided he needed a new direction in his life...

I knock on mum's door – loudly. I can hear the TV in the lounge, as can most of the street in all likelihood. I know she's not going to answer, not with that racket going on, so I let myself in.

Nelson barges past me and unceremoniously transfers his

affections to the weaker of the two – definitely mum every time. She coos at him (pretty pathetic really) and puts out his bowl. It's already filled with left over cottage pie (no wonder he's getting fat) which Nelson proceeds to wolf down without it actually touching the sides.

I plonk myself down and top up my glass with some of mum's wine (better vintage)

This ritual comforts us both – for a while, she can kid herself that my dad's still alive and I can make believe that I'm not a forty something divorcee who's terrified she's going to spend the rest of her life alone.

Like I said, it works.

Wednesday 9 September

O800 I'm already ensconced in the office waiting for the first 'problem.'

The first day after the arrival of the International English Language Trainees NEVER runs smoothly – come to think of it, neither does the second or the third, or the fourth…

The cadets have been shown exactly where to come and are supposed to report promptly at 0830.

0832 We have one Kuwait Coastguard who has found his way (mostly by accident) to the language school. When asked where his colleagues are he shrugs and looks bored (very common response to any question from 'Where do you come from?' to 'How many wives has your father got?')

0845 3 more Kuwaitis and (wonders will never cease) 2 of the 4 Qataris.

0855 We've been informed that our unknown royal will be arriving via helicopter this afternoon (very incognito)

Think John is going to have a coronary.

0910 Another 6 Kuwaitis

0915 The rest of the Kuwaitis and one of the Qataris.

0920 The last of the Qataris finally wanders in with his mobile phone plastered to his ear.

Only 50 minutes late –think it might be a first day record.

Before John can be convicted of manslaughter, I gather them all into a classroom and briskly go through my welcome speech and introduce the teachers: Caroline; Heather; Samantha and Andy (our token male poor sod.)
John has got the cadets booked for uniform fittings at 0930 and I wince a little as I look around – I think the average weight must be around 250 pounds.

Still, not my problem. I leave the little darlings to John and head back in to my office – we won't be seeing them again until after lunch (which could be any time from 1330 to the end of the day.)

1030 I pop down to the Wardroom for a quick coffee if one can ever say 'pop' when referring to a route where the casualties outnumber a war zone...

I see the new VSO from a distance – still can't remember his name, think it might be Ron or something.

He looks over and smiles.

Is that a sign?

1330 Lunch was another write off but I did manage to get Nelson out for a quick jaunt for which he was pathetically grateful and seemed determined to show me at every opportunity by peeing for England. (Not for nothing was he named after one of our greatest heroes.)

I'm now getting ready to inform the Staff Officer Training (SOT – are you getting the hang of this?) that most of the Internationals expected have duly arrived (barring the helicopter stunt). We are still of course waiting for the 6 errant Qataris who, we've been reliably informed, will report to the Language School at 0830 tomorrow morning.

Yeah right.

By some miracle (called John) all the cadets have actually made it back to the language school and are sitting together in one classroom looking decidedly uncomfortable in their new uniforms – blue shirt, navy blue sweater, black trousers and boots, poetically called their 'number 4s.

They will live, eat and sleep in these for the next 14 weeks (except when they're being 'beasted' around the sports field – did I mention they have to be fit to commence officer training?)

We can't group them in to classes until they've been tested, so for the time being they're being lumped together.

Unfortunately this means that the current classroom language is Arabic.

1600 The cadets have been allowed to go back to their cabins (the stampede is anything but regimented – we've got a long way to go) and everyone breathes a sigh of relief that we've got through the first day.

We know that our royal has arrived – mainly due to the noise of the helicopter landing on the Parade Ground right outside the classroom windows…

I wander in to the ILO before I remember that John is no doubt waiting to welcome our illustrious guest, who, we've been told wants to be treated *exactly* the same as everyone else – starting with his mode of transport…

1630 I hold another staff meeting – Nelson graces us with his presence and decides to lie directly in the middle of the small staff room thereby ensuring that everyone has to risk life and limb when they step over him (are there any health and safety issues here?)

We discuss how best to structure tomorrow given that the Language tests won't start until Friday morning and we may well still be missing 6 cadets. We settle on 'Getting To Know You' activities (in English preferably) and split the classes randomly since we don't currently know their level of English.

I leave the teachers to work out their individual 'GTKY' lessons (I know that Samantha's generally involves throwing a ball around the classroom and hopping on one leg which I predict will go down a storm with our Arab friends – I make a mental note to ensure that she doesn't use the classroom directly above the Commodore) and drag Nelson back to my office.

John is back having postponed his highness's uniform fitting until tomorrow. There's been lots of hand shaking but very little verbal communication – John says that HRH has a level of English equivalent to a bog brush...

I groan – how on earth are we going to get him ready for Officer Training in 14 weeks?

Still, I'm determined to be positive – this may just have been a ruse to throw us off the scent concerning his royal connections.

Just like the helicopter...

1715 I've had enough and want to go home.

1725 Arrive in the ferry queue

1740 Still in the ferry queue

1750 Still in the ferry queue – I make a mental note to bring a blanket and pillow tomorrow.

1755 I pull on to the ferry and wave at Kevin the ferry man who is really a bit of a local celebrity as well as being a plumber on the side. The ferry men actually got together to create a calendar a la Chippendale style. Unfortunately I never got to see it – it went underground pretty quickly, but I was reliably informed that Kevin could have been on January February and March all by himself...

We were discussing this fact over drinks in the Royal Castle down in Dartmouth a little while ago only to be tapped on the shoulder by a well dressed lady who primly informed us that we were talking about her husband...

Which pretty quickly put an end to that conversation!

2250 I'm finally in bed having spent the entire evening comatose in front of the TV. Unfortunately due to the fact that I've done absolutely zero, I now can't sleep.

Then I remember that tomorrow's Thursday – Shareholders on the Quarterdeck – and I haven't even worked out what to wear.

I leap out of bed and spend the next 45 minutes rummaging through my wardrobe trying to decide which outfit best fits the description: sassy, sophisticated, sexy and business like.

I decide on my chocolate brown suit. The jacket is fitted (maybe a bit too fitted but it does actually do up). The skirt is a little shorter than my usual but it skims the knee quite nicely and I have some killer heels that do wonders for the backs of my legs and more importantly have been tried and tested on The Floor.

All this for a coffee morning...

I climb back in to bed now pleasantly tired (it's amazing what a spot of exercise can do for you).

My last thoughts are of the new VSO.

Is it a sign?

Thursday 10 September

O830 As predicted, the 6 Qataris are nowhere to be found. John is making frantic phone calls to the Embassy after we've both endured a blistering ear bashing from Commander Naval Training and Education (another mouthful so will refer to him from now on as Commander NTE), the essence of which was, "This is a bloody military training establishment, if they're not here in the next 24 hours, they can bloody well go home."

Now it's certainly not John's fault that the Qatari cadets have failed to arrive. Nor is it mine. But I do understand Commander NTE's frustration. Britain's Defence Diplomacy policy (not to mention the Navy's desperate need for cash) dictates that training Internationals is top priority.

But those who make the policies don't actually have to do the training...

John is assured by the soothing tones of Rashid that the cadets are on their way to Dartmouth this very minute and are scheduled to arrive at the College sometime this afternoon.

He gives me the thumbs up and I breathe a sigh of relief. As long as they arrive sometime today, we can go ahead with the testing tomorrow.

I reflect that we're already nearly at the end of week 1 which only gives us 13 weeks to get these International cadets ready for their Officer Training starting in January.

Thinking about it makes me panic a bit and I wonder what on earth I actually wanted this job for – at least when I was a teacher, the buck stopped with somebody else.

0900 I get on the phone to the Physical Training Instructors over at the gym to organize a fitness assessment for the cadets on Monday. I promise the Chief PTI that the students will report to the gym at 0730.

His response is to snort down the phone – he's done this before I can tell.

Not really much else to say.

1025 Shareholders on the Quarterdeck.

Britannia Royal Naval College (I'll call it BRNC from now on) was built at the turn of the century to resemble a ship, and the magnificent cathedral like Quarterdeck with the Poopdeck balcony overlooking it really is the hub of the College. I love Thursdays when the whole College staff gets together there for coffee and biscuits.
As I walk up the steps towards the imposing entrance, I reflect on the splendour of BRNC. How quickly we begin to take things for granted. It reminds me of an occasion when I'd just started teaching at the College.

Several of us were sitting in the Wardroom during Stand Easy and as we sat, a helicopter landed on the parade ground right next to us. What a spectacle – none of us had ever seen anything quite like it (helicopters not really a regular occurrence in the majority of British Language Schools).

We oohed and aahed and watched its descent, completely enraptured.

Fast forward 6 months later.

Similar scenario, Stand Easy in the Wardroom, helicopter landing.

What did we say?

"Wish the pilot would hurry up and land the bloody thing, it's making a hell of a racket."

Sad really.

The Quarterdeck is off The Corridor and although the floor is made of the same lethal material, for some reason they don't polish it quite so much thereby rendering it slightly less effective for those with suicidal tendencies...

I head towards the queue of people waiting for tea and coffee (served from silver pots by waiters on tables covered with white cloths – all very colonial). As I wait, I glance about to see who's around. I wave to Sarah and other people I know while scanning the crowd for Ron, the new VSO (must stop calling him that – probably not his name).

Is he here?

I can't see him and stifle disappointment, which actually surprises me.

Think it must be a sign...

After grabbing a coffee, I make my way over to Sarah and some of the other lecturers.

I'm absently dunking my coffee just as a voice says "Hi," in my left ear.

Startled, I drop my biscuit into the cup – and inwardly groan. I can't fish it out – not in polite company. I stir the bits around, in an effort to get them to sink and, plastering a polite smile on my face, turn towards the voice.

It's Ron, the new VSO.

"Hi," he repeats. "Don't know if you remember but we were introduced the other day – I'm Rob, the new VSO."
Rob! That's his name – phew, close call.

"Of course I remember." Oh God I'm gushing. I determinedly take a big sip of my coffee only to feel one of the larger bits of biscuit lodge itself in my throat.

Fear of asphyxiation wars briefly with fear of embarrassment – fortunately the fear of death part wins out and I cough and splutter back into my cup. Luckily *Rob* has a tissue and hastily hands it to me before I begin decorating the front of his uniform.

As the coughing subsides, asphyxiation begins to seem the better option. My face is beetroot red and my eyes are watering profusely.

"Er, I think your mascara might be running – either that or you've got a black eye." My humiliation is complete. *Rob* is making no effort to hide his amusement and has a broad grin on his face.

Swallowing an insane urge to burst in to tears, I try to find a non sticky bit of tissue in an effort to wipe underneath my eye without getting bits of gobbed up biscuit in it.

Luckily, the Commander takes that moment to welcome everyone to this week's shareholders.

"Thank you God," I mumble as everyone's attention turns towards him.

I expect *Rob* to move away once the Commander finishes updating everyone with the College news, but he seems quite content to stay where he is.

We chat. He asks me how long I've been working at the College. I want to ask him where he's stashed his wife but haven't got the nerve.

Luckily Sarah comes to the rescue by asking him where his home is.

"I've got a cabin on board; it seemed the easiest thing to do after my wife and I separated last year."

I resist the urge to punch the air and make an effort to look suitably saddened to hear about their break up.

He goes on to tell me enthusiastically about his 7 year old son Jack who lives with his mum in Manchester.

He has a 7 year old son.

How old does that make him?

He doesn't *look* that much younger than me.

But then my youngest is 23 – eek.

I try frantically to think of a way to ask him his age but the Quarterdeck is beginning to empty and I'm forced into a strategic withdrawal.

Live to fight another day as they say.

I murmur a polite goodbye and offer a slight smile (not too friendly but not too frigid either – there's an art to this) then I turn my back and walk away.

Now this I'm good at.

I know, just *know* that he's watching me go, so I walk slowly and deliberately swing my bottom from side to side.

I resist the urge to turn round to see if he's watching – any twisting motion on this floor could result in a double back flip.

And finally exit the stage triumphantly

Think it's definitely a sign…

1115 I get back to the language school where I can hear less than enthusiastic thumping sounds coming from the first classroom.

Shit, I forgot to change Samantha's classroom.

I hurriedly get on the phone to the Commodore's PA, grovelling apology at the ready.

Fortunately the Commodore's up in London until Monday so I breathe a sigh of relief and resolve to ban all physical GTKU exercises from the classroom.

Maybe I should extend that to outside the classroom too – just in case.

1530 Still missing 6 Qataris.

1630 John gets a phone call from HMS Raleigh in Cornwall asking if we know anything about 'training some Arabs.'

Turns out they've gone to the wrong establishment.
Oh well, at least it confirms that they are actually in the Country...

John organizes a mini bus to go and collect them from Raleigh and bring them back to BRNC.

1700 All the tests are locked up in my office and ready to go for tomorrow. I think it's time for a quick drink – the Cherub is calling. I head down the hill with Caroline and John and 15 minutes later we're walking into the welcoming dimness of Dartmouth's oldest pub.

A glass of wine and a portion of chips – complete with mayonnaise and tomato ketchup. It's the small things that make life worth living.

Friday 11 September

O830 It's been a long week.

The language school is quiet as the teachers have all gone off to oversee the English language tests, done in one of the larger classrooms off The Corridor.

We only have 34 students but it takes every teacher we have to ensure that each cadet's contribution is entirely his own. Past experience has taught us that "I help my friend" is a very common concept.

They have their Reading, Writing and Listening tests in the morning which leaves all afternoon for the one to one Speaking tests. And then all hands on deck – nobody goes home until the tests have been marked and the cadets put into the appropriate levels.

In theory, all International Cadets are supposed to have a certain level of English to be accepted into language training at BRNC, otherwise they have no hope of reaching the standard required to undergo Officer Training with the British Cadets.

In theory...

1230 Ok, all the morning tests completed. There was no reported conferring (mostly because the room used can comfortably accommodate around 80 people so we were able to seat them all at least 10 feet apart).

I dish out the completed papers to all the teachers not conducting the speaking tests this afternoon and we head en mass to have a fortifying lunch.

It's going to be a long afternoon.

1245 The Wardroom is always busy on Friday lunchtime. Officers like to come in for their fish and chips before heading back home to their families for the weekend (and as most College functions take place on a Thursday evening, the grease helps to soak up the alcohol consumed the night before...)

The College generally resembles the Marie Celeste on a Friday afternoon.

Normally I try to avoid the fish and chips but decide today to throw caution to the winds and go the whole hog with the lame excuse that I need the 'brain food.' However, I decide to put a bit of salad on my plate to give it a bit more colour.

It's called denial.

1830 5 hours later all the tests are marked and the students grouped according to their English level.

All of them that is apart from one.

It turns out that our resident Royal really does have the English language level of a bog brush...

I sigh.

Thank God it's the weekend.

Sunday 13 September

2100 Sitting with a well deserved glass of wine.
As far as the weekend goes, NTR (Nothing To Report –just *had* to get that in…)

In other words pretty normal really. Went for a spot of retail therapy yesterday although it didn't really provide much in the way of therapy as I only went in to Torquay which is the retail equivalent of the Gobi Desert.

Had lunch at the Boathouse today with my sister Jackie – it's the nearest thing we've got to a local. It's on the beach, so we get to walk the dogs and have a reward for our efforts.

Like me, my sister's divorced. Her marriage broke up when her husband had an affair 10 years ago ("You've got to realise Jackie that I have a new life now – you need to go out and get one for yourself.")

Like that's possible with kids of 10 and 3.

So, Sunday lunch time we drink wine, assess the week and bitch about anything and everything.

It's all very therapeutic.

And Sunday night is family night with all 3 generations taking part. Everyone sits around the table at either my sister's or mine and basically whoever shouts the loudest gets heard.

I love it.

Tonight it was at mine and Frankie did the dinner. As I said earlier, Frankie's idea of cooking basically involves using every pan and dish in the kitchen and leaving me to clear up the wreckage.

Always tastes good though – her long term ambition is to own her own café and I think she'd do brilliantly, (providing she has a dishwasher that doesn't include me).

I did actually think briefly about suggesting she apply for a job going at BRNC but really don't think they'd get on. Frankie's idea of pomp and ceremony is to avoid breaking wind in public!

So now I'm enjoying a few minutes of peace and quiet before bed. Everyone's left and it's just me and Nelson.

I think about Rob and wonder if he really could be Mr Right finally turning up on cue.

Week 2 should be interesting…

Week 2

Monday 14 September

O745 So here we are, Monday of Week 2 and I'm in the office early – all fired up and ready.

This is when the real training starts. We now have 13 weeks to get the International Officer Cadets ready to undertake the Royal Navy's Young Officer Course commencing in January.

I feel a bit sick and wonder what on earth we're going to do with His Royal Highness. His father's not just any old sheikh (believe me there are lots of those). This one's the brother to the King.

Bloody defence diplomacy…

I'm going to have to report the issue asap to Commander NTE – really it's his problem.

Problem is he prefers it to be mine.

0750 I get a phone call from the PTIs at the gym. It seems that only 3 of the cadets have turned up for their fitness test.

Surprise surprise…

I phone John's mobile; luckily he's on his way in – he'll drag the rest of the sleeping beauties out of bed.

I decide it's time for my first caffeine fix. I have an unfinished packet of ginger nuts in my drawer and Nelson's not going to leave me alone until I give him one. He may be a croissant short of a continental breakfast in most things, but he's a veritable blood hound when it comes to scenting out biscuits!

1030 Ok, all students have finished their fitness tests and are now in their correct classrooms with their correct teachers – it's time to rock and roll...

Think I'll go for another coffee.

1100 I come back to a bit of a commotion. One of the Qataris is refusing to walk past Nelson on the off chance that the crazed beast might jump up and bite him. The culprit is sitting on the floor regarding the cadet with his tail wagging furiously.

I drag him back into my office admonishing him sternly – he knows he's not to wander around the language school on his own (Nelson that is, not the cadet...)

1130 I have a meeting with Commander NTE which I'm really not looking forward to.

I sit chatting with his PA for a few minutes while he finishes up with his 11o'clock; takes me back to my school days and being sent to sit outside the Headmaster's office (not that it happened *that* regularly). A lot of the naval officers I've met have a tendency to actually sound like my old headmaster – although in fairness I remember him being red haired and balding and I have to admit that the current Commander NTE is really quite attractive.

Just need to remember I'm not one of his sailors...

1230 I head down to the Wardroom for lunch – and not just salad. Preferably something with chips.

The meeting with Commander NTE did not go well.

He knows it's not my fault that HRH's English is not only not good enough to get him onto a Military English language course, it isn't actually good enough to ask for a hamburger in McDonalds.

And I know it's not his.

Unfortunately we haven't really got anyone else we can bitch to.

Maybe HRH will be a quick learner!

Tentative murmurs hinting our concerns will be made to his Embassy.

Hope the Ambassador's English is a bit better…

1300 Eaten a suitably stodgy lunch known in posh Military Circles as 'cheesy, hammy, eggy' (pretty self explanatory) and finishing off with a fruit tea in an effort to stave off the resulting indigestion which I know is on its way any minute now.

Rob is sitting with a group of officers in the cluster of easy chairs adjacent to me and although I keep my eyes glued determinedly to my newspaper, I can feel that he keeps glancing over.

I wonder if he's going to the Wardroom Happy Hour on Thursday.

Also wonder what he did at the weekend. Now the wife issue is out of the way, I really do need to check out possible partners and girlfriends. Oh God, what if he's gay?

I glance up involuntarily to find him staring at me.

No, he's definitely not gay.

Must be a sign…

Tuesday 15 September

O 800 I called a staff meeting early this morning so we can get it in before the cadets arrive on the dot at 0830 (yeah right).

Quick first impressions?

All 8 Kuwait Navy Cadets and 7 of the Kuwait Coastguard seem to be taking the whole thing pretty seriously – might be because their authorities make them pay back the cost of the training if they fail...
8 Kuwait Coastguard seem to think it doesn't matter whether they fail or not because their parents are so rich that they can pay back the training costs easily.

All 10 Qatar Coastguard prefer to believe they are at a finishing school for Middle Eastern aristocracy. ("What, you mean this is *actually* a military establishment?")

And as for our incognito royal...

We decide immediately that HRH will need additional 1 to 1 coaching (really?) Particularly since his Embassy are either refusing to believe that a potential heir to the throne could be anything less than perfect in every way or admitting it could potentially see them whisked back home for 50 lashes and a 30 year stint digging drains in the desert!

There also appears to be another problem.

John says that HRH doesn't know how to do up the buttons on his shirt – it appears he's never had to do it before. Currently getting dressed in the morning is taking him over an hour and he ends up looking like an extra from a Norman Wisdom film.

And he doesn't even know what an iron is.

This, I determine loudly (and even a little hysterically) is absolutely NOT our problem. The RN can handle it. I tell John to report the problem to Chief May (poetically known in military circles as Daisy).

"It's not really his..." I cut him off before he can go any further by slamming down my notebook and glaring at him (I can do angry when I'm, well, angry.)

"I don't care whether it's his part of ship or not John, just do it." (I think I've been here too long, I'm actually starting to sound like a naval officer).

John wisely decides not to pursue the subject – he can see I'm a little irate...

And that pretty much puts an end to the meeting. I gather my notes and sweep out of the room (I know it's not 'Gone With The Wind', but sometimes a situation calls for a little drama.)

My exit would have been perfect if not for Nelson who's lying across the doorway and decides to raise his head just as I'm stepping over him.

A dog's nose up your skirt is so not Scarlett O'Hara!

1030 Stand Easy time. I can hear the cadets stamping down the corridor in anything but military precision – their Ceremonial Training should be fun, but at least we don't have to do it.

I'm eternally grateful that our 'part of ship' is purely the language training.

I head down the Language School stairs and come out onto the flat area fronting the offices of the shakers and movers in the College – The Commodore who's the overall head of the College; The Commander who's responsible for the day to day running of the College and Commander Naval Training and Education who I have most to do with (lucky me) and who's responsible for the Training and Education (obviously).

I'm just about to go down the next flight of stairs to take my chances on The Corridor when Rob emerges from Commander NTE's office along with his opposite number – Cunningham Senior Squadron Officer (amazingly known as CSO). Did I mention that the 2 squadron heads work very closely together?

The new CSO is a woman...

And they're laughing together.

Bugger – hope it's not a sign.

I pretend that I haven't seen them and hobble down the stairs as quickly as my heels will allow. Unfortunately it's not quick enough and to top it all I lose my shoe on the second to last step.

Swearing under my breath I turn and limp back to the stupid thing just as they're coming round the bend in the stairs.

"Hi Bev," Rob calls and I glance up as if I've only just spotted them, holding up the offending shoe with a gay 'look what silly me's done' laugh. I'm aiming for a sort of giggle but it comes out more as a cackle with a very unladylike snort at the end.

Why the bloody hell do I wear these things? That's it, tomorrow I'm wearing trainers.

Rob gets to the bottom of the stairs just as I get my shoe back on and enthusiastically introduces me to the new CSO Anna.

She looks as happy to see me as I am to see her and after looking me up and down with an 'Oh God not another civvy expression, (I can tell she's not in the mood for an extended chat) she gives a quick nod and pulls Rob's arm towards the Wardroom announcing that she 'dying' for a coffee.

"Coming Bev?" Rob calls over his shoulder as he's being marched away.

There is absolutely no way that I can negotiate this floor at the speed they are going.

So I smile brightly and wave them on before heading in to the planning office opposite as though that had been my destination all along.

I'm quite happy to spend my Stand Easy bitching to Sarah.

1100 I come out of Sarah's office with my good humour completely restored.

Turns out that one of the computer techs walked in on Jemma Matthews while she was shagging one of the officers over a desk in an unused office.

He thinks he might require therapy (the computer tech that is, not the officer).

The officer's more likely to be requiring a transfer…

1230 I decide against going to the Wardroom for lunch in the interests of (a) keeping myself slightly aloof and off limits to certain people and (b) my diet.

I swap my heels for sturdy walking boots and walk Nelson round the college grounds instead. Look a bit ridiculous with my suit and nylons but there's no one to see me.

Unfortunately on my way back I run into Rob returning from the gym.

Bugger. So much for aloof and mysterious – very difficult to achieve when you're wearing gum boots and dragging a 60lb

Irish terrier.

He doesn't laugh though and he does like dogs

It must be a sign...

1500 John has spoken to the Powers That Be about HRH's problems dressing himself and it's been decided to assign him a British Officer Cadet who will help show him the ropes - which presumably will include the basics in button fastening and ironing.

I wonder which poor sod has been nominated and exactly what he did to warrant it.

Wednesday 16 September

O930 I love Wednesdays. It's our lightest day in terms of teaching and we get the opportunity to lift our heads above the parapet – and not just to get it shot off. We're able to take stock of what's working (and more importantly what isn't).

The cadets are not into class until after Stand Easy because they're having their first boat driving lesson on the River Dart with Chief May.

Then the afternoon is given over to whole College sports. That means *every* cadet, including the Internationals.

While the cadets are on the river, we have a staff meeting to discuss the possibility of introducing more specific 'military' language into the 14 week curriculum.

One of the pivotal points in the cadets' Officer Training is ABLE – an Assessed Basic Leadership Exercise conducted on Dartmoor. Basically the idea is that cadets are taken to one of the bleakest and most inhospitable places in the UK, pushed to their limits in terms of hunger and exhaustion in order to test their leadership mettle in adverse conditions (a bit like going to Morrison's really...)

They carry rations, sleep outside for 3 days and spend each day tramping around Dartmoor carrying packs the size of a small pony, undertaking various training exercises during which

41

they're assessed and ultimately passed or failed.

If they fail, they might be given a second chance, depending on how catastrophic the failure was, but after that, a second failure is curtains as far as a career in the Royal Navy is concerned.

So pretty important really.

Obviously we want to be able to prepare the International Cadets as much as possible in terms of language for the challenges they'll have to face.
So we've appealed to the RN Leadership Training Department to allow us to go up on to Dartmoor with the cadets to observe the training first hand. ABLE generally takes place in Week 7 which gives us 4 weeks grace to organize the trip.

Obviously we'll only go up for the day – we really don't need to experience the hunger and exhaustion bit. I'm really quite excited by the whole idea (obviously – it was mine).

For some reason the Leadership department don't seem quite so thrilled…

1100 The International Cadets are trickling in less than enthusiastically after their first experience afloat. One of them in particular is looking very green (there aren't any waves in the Gulf).

Chief May follows the last cadet in and comes in to my office to 'report' which generally involves a cup of tea and a custard cream – it's no wonder I can't lose weight).

He reports no major catastrophes (which means basically that no one fell in…)

1225 Andy marches in to my office after a curt "Wait outside," to someone I can't see – I'm assuming that it's one of his students and my heart sinks – I was hoping that we'd get to week 3 before I had to start dishing out lectures.

Apparently one of the cadets fell asleep during the lesson. (Nothing new there really.)

Andy brings him in to my office for said lecture.

He's a Qatari so it's no use starting with the softly, softly approach – you know, try to appeal to their sense of pride and how important it is to their families that they do well, blah, blah, blah…

I cut straight to where it hurts most.

I tell the cadet that he will not be allowed to leave the College this weekend.

That means no trip up to London. Fate worse than death.

I ruthlessly cut him off before we get in to the "But ma'am my mother/father/brother/uncle/4th cousin is flying over especially to see me *this* weekend and I absolutely *have* to get to London."
As he trails disconsolately from the room looking as though he might cry at any minute, I go into the ILO to tell John my decision (and to forestall any appeal in that direction).

See, I'm not always a push over…

1230 I don't feel like going to the Wardroom for lunch so I take Nelson out for a walk instead. Despite my bravado, I really don't like disciplining the cadets but I know from experience that it has to be nipped in the bud.
If you give them an inch, they take a mile (or a flight home).

1330 The language school is peaceful and quiet. I take a deep breath for a second then let it out slowly. I can hear the murmur of teachers working on their lessons and the occasional shout from the rugby pitch but that's all.

Bliss.

As a general rule most Middle Eastern Internationals seem to regard sport in much the same vein as the prospect of eating pork – with absolute horror.

Nevertheless, this afternoon the International Cadets in English Language Training are being shown the ropes, taken through their paces and impressed upon that the Wednesday afternoon sporting options do not include going to bed!

I wonder how HRH is going on…

1710 I got loads done this afternoon and am consequently feeling very virtuous as I walk towards the car.

Only one of the internationals attempted to get out of afternoon sports by hiding under his bed which I think is actually pretty impressive. That makes 2 of them staying on board this weekend…

1715 I filter in to the ferry queue resolutely ignoring the chap in the car behind me beeping his horn furiously because I got in first (I'm tempted to flip him a finger but really don't want to be dragged out of the car by a possible axe wielding maniac suffering from ferry rage…)

1725 Still in the ferry queue. I close my eyes and prepare myself for a spot of meditation (mostly because every time I inadvertently glance in my rear view mirror I have an up close and personal view of the potential maniac still glaring at me in the car behind).

I can feel a headache coming on.

Thursday 17 September

O800 I have my overnight bag because I'm staying on board tonight due to the first 'Happy Hour' of the term. These usually take place about once a month and are a chance for all the members of the Wardroom Mess to get together, have a bite to eat and a drink.

Mostly drink – hence the overnight bag.

Negotiating The Corridor with a holdall and Nelson in tow is no mean feat.

I stand for a moment at the entrance near to the Chapel and juggle my overnight bag, handbag and dog.

Nelson looks at me and I swear he has a grin on his face.

Ok, handbag on right shoulder. Overnight bag in left hand. Nelson on *very* short lead being held in a death grip in my right hand.

I'm ready to go.

Within 10 feet the handbag has fallen off my shoulder straight on top of Nelson's head who goes down as if he's been pole axed (it's only got my make up in it...)

I'm within a hairs breadth of going the same way, complete with probable broken ankle and/or serious head injury, but at the 11th hour my survival instincts kick in and I let go of everything.

Nelson goes tearing off down the corridor with his lead trailing behind him.

Unfortunately my hand bag is still attached to said lead and consequently my makeup, mobile phone, car keys, hair brush and other contents of the offending bag (oh God is that a tampon?) are now littering the corridor behind him...

There's no alternative: I grab my overnight bag, take off my shoes and stuff them inside. Then I zigzag down the corridor in my stocking feet picking up my belongings.
Anybody watching will think I'm either drunk or doing the salsa (probably both).

The only positive is that the skirt I'm wearing today is well below my knees (well it was when I started).

It's also still early so no one is around to witness the commotion *and* Nelson knows where he's going.

By the time I get to my office I feel as though I've done a 200 metre sprint – come to think of it, I probably have. I collapse into my chair and glare at Nelson who is busy scratching behind his ear with complete unconcern.

I'm definitely wearing trainers next week.

1030 I head to the Quarterdeck for Shareholders. Sarah and I are taking the opportunity to discuss life defining issues such as which cabins we have been allotted for tonight; what we intend to wear to the happy hour and whether she has remembered to bring a bottle of wine complete with screw top and 2 glasses to help with the ritual of getting ready. (After the fiasco this morning I give thanks that I didn't attempt a dog, an overnight bag, a hand bag *and* a bottle of wine.)

I look around for Rob but can't see him milling around the quarterdeck or waiting in the coffee queue.

I am actually really disappointed

That's definitely a sign.

I hope he's going to be at the happy hour tonight.

1050 I get back to the Language School to find the 2 Qataris banned from leaving the College this weekend waiting outside. Knowing that any appeal to my better nature could actually take awhile, I tell them to go in to class and I'll see them before they go off to lunch.

The hope in their eyes makes me feel like I've just given them a last minute reprieve from a death sentence.

The College really isn't that bad...

1225 I sit and listen to the excuses as to why they fell asleep in class/spent Wednesday afternoon under the bed which, as far as I could tell with their limited English, (did I say we've got a long way to go?) revolved around having been tired due to spending an inordinate amount of time on their homework the 2 evenings before.

"Did you actually finish the homework?" I ask, knowing full well neither had handed in any of the homework set for this week.

"Of course ma'am," they assured me earnestly, hurt that I could ask such a thing.

"Then I'll speak to your teachers tomorrow after they've had chance to mark your work and I'll make a decision then. Come and see me during your break tomorrow afternoon."

"But tomorrow is Friday ma'am."

I nod my head and mention how pleased I am that they can remember the days of the week in English. Then, ignoring the slightly panicked look in their eyes which confirms what I already know about the homework front (and before they can give me any more 'buts'), I dismiss them and turn back to my desk trying hard not to smile.

They really are very sweet.

1630 It's been a long afternoon. We've had 3 more students fall asleep in class which brings us to a total of 5 staying in the College over the weekend and to finish the afternoon off nicely, it appears that HRH has misunderstood slightly the role of the British cadet assigned to him. John had to explain at length and with lots of hand waving that said cadet's duties do not include steam cleaning HRH's silk shirts…

1640 I definitely need some fresh air so I decide to call it a day and take Nelson out for a bit of a jaunt seeing as he'll be spending the majority of his evening snoozing in my cabin.

1700 Nelson's business taken care of, I give Sarah a quick ring to tell her I'm heading up to my cabin.

The sleeping accommodation at BRNC is situated high up in what only can be described as a long narrow attic accessed through a maze of corridors which are almost impossible to find unless you know where you're going, so after this morning's performance I decide to make this a 2 stage operation – first taking up my bags then coming back down to the office for Nelson.

10 minutes and at least 200 calories burned later I'm finally sitting in my cabin getting my breath back.

The good thing about the fact that the guest cabins are so high up is that you do have a fantastic view over the Parade Ground and the River Dart from the majority.
On the negative side, if you suffer from claustrophobia, you're very likely to have the worst night's sleep of your life. The cabins could not be described by even the most tolerant critic as 'hotel accommodation'. A closer description would be Prisoner Cell Block H complete with 2 foot beds and scratchy woolen blankets

covering starched cotton sheets that are tucked in so tightly you need a crowbar to extract yourself. And don't forget the communal bathrooms...

All very character building.

Just doesn't bode well for a good night's sleep (especially when sharing your bed with a dog who could give Beethoven a run for his money).

To be fair, consuming copious amounts of wine before getting into bed doesn't help either.

I decide to have a nice hot bath while I'm waiting for Sarah.

I've been lucky with my cabin selection this time and getting to the nearest bathroom only involves a 50 metre sprint as opposed to an exercise that would do justice to an episode of Mission Impossible in order to avoid half the College sniggering at the sight of me in my dressing gown.

And the baths are actually in private cubicles – another bonus.

I remember when I was pregnant many eons ago and the nurse asked me if I wanted a nice hot bath to relax me. What she didn't tell me was that the cavernous bathroom was actually a short cut for all the doctors and nurses working in the maternity ward. So I sat like a beached whale in 6 inches of tepid water making small talk to every Tom Dick and Harry passing through in a white coat.

It was the longest half an hour of my life. The bath was in the middle of the room and my towel was about 20 feet away – it might as well have been in another country.

Memories...

I only spend 20 minutes in the bath. The Happy Hours usually kick off about 18.30 plus I'm gagging for a glass of wine.

I get back to my cabin to find that Sarah bless her has already preempted me and a large glass of rosé is sitting waiting for me on the window sill. Nelson is already snoring, taking up 90% of the bed – he'll only rouse himself now for his dinner and a last wee.

Oh to be a dog.

1830 I take a last critical look in the mirror. I think I'll pass muster.

I'm wearing black Capri pants with my favourite black and white heels - ok they're not quite Jimmy Choo (more New Look really) but they make my ankles look really good! And over the top a simple fitted white shirt showing a little bit of cleavage – mostly it has to be said because the button won't do up over my chest.

My makeup is subtle – I'm going for the 'girl next door' casual look (which as we all know takes half a ton foundation and a 20 week course in cosmetic science to achieve...)

But you know what? The end result is pretty good if I say so myself.

1835 Sarah and I are ready to head down to the Wardroom after finishing off the bottle of wine (obviously a crime to waste it).

It is in fact possible to get nearly all the way to the Wardroom from the guest cabins without actually stepping foot on The Corridor – it does take twice as long but nevertheless substantially increases the probability of arriving at your destination in one piece (providing you don't fall down the stairs of course.)

1845 I push open the door and stand for a moment watching all the uniform staff milling around the Wardroom with its stunning backdrop of the River Dart and Dartmouth in the distance below and reflect again how lucky I am to be able to work (and play) in such amazing surroundings.

"Hey Bev, Sarah what are you drinking?" Instantly snapping out of my reverie, I turn towards Sam, the cute new Training

Executive Officer (otherwise known as TXO) waving at us from the bar.

Let the fun begin...

Most social functions at BRNC really *are* great fun, particularly as the one thing that Naval Officers are good at (of course it's not the *only* thing) is small talk. Diplomacy is a vital part of their training and it's essential they remember that they are representing the British Government at all times and in all situations (never seems to put a damper on their alcohol consumption though –see, there's another thing they're good at).

Sarah and I spend the next hour chatting (ok maybe flirting just a little) with several officers while taking advantage of the chips laid out on the bar (starting the diet on Monday – can't possibly begin at the weekend).

Rob hasn't arrived yet, and, as my cunning plan consists of looking as though I really don't give a hoot whether he's there or not, I resolutely turn my back on the door...

1950 Damn it Rob still hasn't arrived – beginning to think he's not going to show. CSO Anna is here (which goes to prove that at least they're not joined at the hip)

I keep glancing towards the door. Although I'm obviously trying to do it unobtrusively - which is really difficult when you're facing the opposite way. I sense the officer I'm chatting to is beginning to think I've got a particularly severe nervous twitch.

2000 At last success. Rob has just walked through the door. He's wearing his number 2s signifying that he's Officer of the Day. His lateness is explained – he's been inspecting the cadets.

He looks like he's going to a ball – sometimes all this pomp and circumstance feels so over the top – but actually as I watch him stride to the bar, I stifle a small shiver.

He looks yummy.

Most definitely a sign…

2230 There is a girlfriend

Bugger, bugger, bugger, bugger, bugger, bugger, bugger

Her name's Tracy and he spent 7 minutes and 38 seconds talking about her (I was looking at the clock behind his head).

And to top it all she's 23…

Maybe Rob's not Mr Right after all. I still don't know his age but know he's definitely younger than me. If he has a 23 year old girlfriend, why on earth would he be remotely interested in a 46 year old woman with 2 grown up kids?

Maybe I'm doomed to spend the rest of my life sharing a bed with a snoring, dribbling, farting dog (although come to think of it, that actually describes most men too – makes me feel a bit better).

I give Nelson an experimental shove. I might as well have been trying to move a four foot tree trunk.

I sense it's going to be a long night.

Friday 18 September

O730 Spent the whole night pinned up against the wall. Never again – next time I stay on board, Nelson can stay with Frankie!

I was awake at 6am (and 4 and 3 and 1) so by 6.30 I decided enough was enough and made a concerted effort to get out of bed.

By the time I'd extracted myself, I felt like I could've given Houdini a run for his money.

A quick walk, cup of coffee and 2 ginger nuts later, I'm sat at my computer feeling pretty jaded and low, which I keep telling myself has nothing to do with a certain officer and everything to do with lack of sleep.

Think it's time to bring out the big guns. I have no option but to pay a visit to the College shop (otherwise known as the Naafi) and buy a packet of donuts.

0830 Now feeling sick in addition to jaded and low, although I have the small consolation that I didn't actually eat all 4 of the donuts – I gave one to Nelson.

The cadets are beginning to filter up the stairs and a queue is already forming outside my office door. I have to say I'm not feeling particularly charitable.

I fling open the office door (well actually 'fling' is probably a bit dramatic as it's a fire door and flinging it open would challenge a finalist in The World's Strongest Woman competition). Still, the cadets waiting there were gratifyingly startled; one even dropped his mobile phone (no mean feat seeing as most of them appear to have their phones surgically implanted in their left ear).

I tell the cadets that I need to speak with their teacher before I make a final decision regarding their weekend leave and that they will be informed of my decision at 15.30 – not a moment before.

They reluctantly shuffle off to class and I resolve to hide between now and the moment I put them out of their misery. I have no intention of letting them off the hook – if I do, I'm simply showing my weakness as a woman and they'll walk all over me (and of course I run a tight ship...)

The problem is, if I tell them my decision now, it gives them another 7 hours to plead, beg and offer me all kinds of bribes (ok maybe I should consider telling them sooner).

At the end of the day, they'll be miserable but they'll also know I mean business.

1300 I head down to the Wardroom even though I don't really want anything to eat – the donuts are still sitting like a lead weight in my stomach. I grab some fruit (I'm really good at martyrdom) and a coffee and tuck myself away in a corner with the newspaper.

Rob doesn't come in and I torture myself with thoughts that he's even now driving off to be with his 23 year old nymphomaniac. They can't possibly have anything in common, but then they probably don't talk much...

Sometimes I hate my imagination

1550 My popularity has reached an all time low. I have informed the cadets that there will be no last minute reprieve and given them instructions to spend their weekend focusing on the homework that they have so far failed to do.

It's taken a good 20 minutes to get them all out of my office – it's tragic the number of relatives they have in London who are virtually on their deathbeds...

However, I feel sorrier for the teachers who have to take them for their last lesson.

1615 I decide I've had enough for the day (and the week) plus, if I leave now I'll avoid the accusing and reproachful looks of the condemned 5 as they come out of their classrooms.

I've already put my overnight gear into the car (see I do learn). Nelson is making it blatantly obvious he's not keen on moving (the clue being his total refusal to get off the chair) so I bribe him with a dog biscuit, put on his lead and start the trek to the car park.

1630 There is a God.

I bumped in to Rob on the way to the car; he was just heading off for the weekend.

He seemed really pleased to see me and we stood chatting for a while. Turns out he's not going to his girlfriend's; he's actually going to spend the weekend with his son Jack.

Apparently his girlfriend is not keen on the three of them spending time together...

Which is a really good reason why he might prefer a 46 year old divorcee as opposed to a 23 year old bimbo.

Think it's definitely a sign...

Saturday 19 September

O930 The weather outside is pants so I've decided to indulge in a well earned lie in. Have taken Nelson for a wee and we're now snuggled up sharing some toast and marmite and listening to the rain.

Think I might need to bath him later...

2300 Bit of an embarrassing evening really. Been raining all day so decided to go to the cinema with sister Jackie plus best friends Sally and Debbie.

Of course this involved a drink first (who goes to the pics without having a drink first...?)

Unfortunately this meant we missed the start (including preview time – my favourite bit). Naturally due to the crappy weather everyone else and his dog also decided to head to the cinema which meant we got split up. I sat with Sally while Jackie sat with Debbie on the row in front.

I thought they were directly in front of us, so for a bit of a laugh (always a mistake when you've had a couple of glasses of wine) I leant forward and patted my sister on the shoulder. "You've got a big head" I said in a loud stage whisper giggling, just before noticing that Jackie was actually sitting two seats down.

"What did that woman say?"

"She said I've got a big head."

I was mortified. Shrinking down in my seat, I spent the next 2 hours trying to gauge how tall the woman I'd insulted would be when she stood up; what possible excuse I could give for my rude comments concerning the size of her head and whether she had a leaning towards casual violence.

The other three spent the time sniggering...

Sunday 20 September

Today has been a complete write off – have spent the whole day at work.

I was just getting ready to walk down to the Boathouse to meet Jackie when I received a message from John that HRH was refusing to return to BRNC after informing his Embassy that he had contracted 'Ham' flu at the College.

A flurry of panicked phone calls from said Embassy (and HRH's mother) followed this announcement and it took four bloody hours of repeated assurances that there were currently no cases of 'Swine' Flu at BRNC to persuade his royalness that it was safe to return to such a breeding ground of insidious germs!

Finally, at 5pm it was decided that HRH would spend the night in a private (and very expensive) Harley Street clinic (under observation!) and return to BRNC in the morning.

Not quite sure when 'incognito' went out of the window.

Bring on Week 3…

Week 3

Monday 21 September

1230 HRH has not yet arrived back in the College but we're assured that he has been discharged from his private clinic and will be chauffeur driven back to BRNC sometime this afternoon...

Beginning to get the feeling he might just be intending to milk this for all it's worth.

Still, I have more important things to think about than our incognito royal because I found out in the Wardroom during stand easy this morning that we have one of our own royals coming! Apparently we're getting a visit from Prince Charles – The Prince of Wales no less – in just a couple of weeks; and, even more exciting, I've been asked if I'd like to meet him.

"Hell, yes," was of course my answer.

So now I'm on a strict diet. I've got 15 days to get to Drop Dead Gorgeous.

Which is why I'm about to put my trainers on (this really is serious) and drag Nelson round the perimeter of the College grounds - at least a mile and a half I'm sure. (You didn't actually think I was going to the gym did you? Don't be silly – I really don't do red, hot and sweaty – well, maybe in certain circumstances but definitely not on a running machine...)

1315 Actually beginning to think that the gym might have been preferable to dragging a 62Ib Irish terrier (think he's put on weight) on what felt like a 10 mile hike. Nelson does sniffing, peeing and standing really well. He *doesn't* do brisk walking.

That said, I'm sure my arms must have benefitted from the extra pulling – bit like doing press ups.

So now I'm sitting in my office (looking a *little* red and sweaty it has to be said) contemplating a packet of 'Italian' salad which to the uninitiated looks like something out of Gardeners Weekly.

It tastes disgusting. I really don't mind salad but usually prefer something with it such as pizza.

Still, it's in a good cause – I mustn't lose sight of the objective.
Mind you, I read somewhere that lettuce is poisonous – think maybe tomorrow I'll opt for a Weight Watchers Ready Meal – I think I've got one lurking in the freezer somewhere.

1600 HRH has finally arrived back in the College in a chauffeured limousine along with his Ambassador – not sure if the latter was there to ensure that the prince had no momentary lapses or to make sure that he didn't try to do a runner..

Still the poor love did look a bit pale while we were serving tea and biscuits in my office (not that it stopped him wolfing down the rest of my custard creams, though I made sure that he didn't get a chance at my secret stash of ginger nuts).

Unfortunately my office is fairly small so it was pretty cramped; particularly since Nelson - completely exhausted from his earlier marathon - was comatose in the middle of the floor and totally unresponsive to either custard cream (must have been knackered) or a hefty kick.

Luckily our little tea party was cut short as the Ambassador was due to call on the Commodore.
John took HRH back to his cabin and the Ambassador promised to check up on him before leaving (definitely making sure his royalness not intending to do a runner).

It was made perfectly clear that he will be expected in class tomorrow morning (HRH, not the Ambassador...)

1705 I've got a great book so quite happy to sit in the ferry queue today (it also helps me to avoid thinking about food).

I've always been a keen reader, honing my skills during my younger years on the myriad of 'bodice rippers' that were so popular (and still are). I remember giving Rosie (my eldest) and Frankie a particularly lurid romance in an effort to get them reading when they were in their teens. It got them reading alright but I then had to explain that love making does not *necessarily* include multiple orgasms involving Adonis like men with 6 packs and tackle the size of a donkey.

Better to let them down gently...

Luckily they loved reading and have since graduated to the likes of John Grisham.

And I've graduated to Harry Potter.

Although mustn't forget that very occasionally I actually read books that are reviewed by the Daily Telegraph...

Mind you, literary aspirations aside, maybe I should just re-read a couple of the juicier books, so I don't forget how it's done when the time comes.

...Nah, think I'll stick with The Deathly Hallows and trust that my libido can find its way out of the deep dark hole it's currently residing in when the appropriate moment comes – which my gut tells me is going to be this year – yey.

Well, under normal circumstances it would – at the moment it's just telling me my throat's been cut...

1850 Feeling very virtuous after eating steamed chicken and brown rice and now just relaxing with a glass of wine. (Did think I'd try giving up alcohol on this diet but on the other hand it's important to drink plenty of fluids.)

2300 Finally found the solitary Weight Watchers meal in the back of the freezer. Not sure how long it's been there but it was definitely frozen solid (actually frozen to the back of the freezer drawer but I managed to pry it off – never let it be said that I have no willpower).

And (bonus) it's a lasagne so I can have it with the rest of the salad tomorrow.

Tuesday 22 September

O 900 I don't think I'm ever going to come out of my office again. They'll probably find me here mummified in 50 years time sitting on top of a bag of canine bones covered in faded ginger fur with my hands around what had once been its throat...

I look over at Nelson who is actually having the good grace to look sheepish – as well he should after what he did to me this morning.

I can hardly bring myself to put this down on paper – I am so mortified.

So what happened?

Well, I decided to come into the College a different way this morning (no idea why but for the record – thank you God!) My route took me along a back corridor which leads onto the Poopdeck balcony overlooking the Quarterdeck.

Nelson and I had had a quick jaunt to give him chance to do his business (wasn't that quick actually – he's a man and the never ending stopping, starting and sniffing is the equivalent to him reading the paper while he thinks about it).

Well, eventually he performed, I picked up the offending pile - with a doggy bag obviously - and popped it into the nearest dog bin.

Ok (I thought) we can head to the office now.

So there we were, doing a fairly good pace along the corridor, just about to go through the glass doors leading onto the Poopdeck when suddenly the mutt from hell starts slowing down.

And sniffing.

And then, horror of horrors, he actually started squatting. He *never* does that *inside*...

I didn't know whether to keep dragging him in the hope that it would put him off or to shove a bag under his backside in the hope that what he produced would land inside it.

While all this was running through my mind, I was chanting 'Oh my God; Oh my God; Oh my God...

Helplessly I watched as a big lump of dog doo landed on the polished floor.

This could not be happening. I started frantically digging in my bag while checking that no one was coming.

And as if things couldn't possibly get any worse, I realised at that moment that I HAD NO MORE BAGS...

What in God's name was I going to do now? I felt sick (if I'd got as far as the Poopdeck, I'd have shoved Nelson off it!) I glanced through the glass doors and could see someone coming towards me.

Shit, shit, shit (pardon the pun).

All I could find in my bag was a screwed up paper tissue.

I had no choice.

Taking a deep breath, I bent down and (using the tissue) picked up the offending lump and plonked it into my handbag....

....On top of the Weight Watchers lasagne...

...Just as the doors to the Poopdeck swung open to reveal Sam the new TXO (on this occasion Execution would definitely have been the better title).

"Just keep walking, *please* just keep walking," I chanted to myself while using my elbow to cover the open top of the bag as well as the offending smell emanating from it...

No such luck.

"Hi Bev, hi Nelson," He smiled coming over to stroke the evil hound – who actually had the temerity to wag his tail.

"Hi Sam." I actually yelled it, causing him to pause his patting and glance up slightly startled.

The disgusting smell was beginning to waft its way into the air and I could see Sam beginning to frown as the odour reached him.

"Gotta go," I continued loudly, dragging Nelson towards the Poopdeck doors which I pushed open so hard that they swung back and hit the traitorous mutt on the nose just as he was about to come through.

Gritting my teeth, I pulled at the door and dragged him through. "Serves you right," I hissed marching him along the Poopdeck. Looking behind I could see Sam still standing looking a little bewildered through the glass doors.

Great, he probably thinks I'm a complete nutcase with a particularly unpleasant strain of body odour.

Luckily I didn't bump in to anyone else before reaching the language school (although I'm sure the hideous miasma must have followed in my wake for some time).

Once there I was able to tip the offending lump in to the toilet and flush, not to mention scrubbing my hands within an inch of their lives...

My lasagne went into the bin.

1030 I can't face Stand Easy.

I picture Sam telling everyone about my 'BO' problem: "My God it was disgusting, do you think we should tell her…?"

I groan into my hands and toy with idea of resigning.
Maybe it'll be possible to just do my job from in here – it's not *really* necessary to mix with people…

1230 It's no good, I've got to come out. Not only am I bloody starving but I need a wee and I'm absolutely not eating the wilting salad I've got left over from yesterday – I'm too traumatised.

I toy with the idea of getting something to eat from the Naafi and spend the next 10 minutes devising a route to get there avoiding all human contact.

Oh God, what if Sam tells Rob that he thinks I've got a problem. Any potential romance could be over before it's even begun.

I simply have to brave the Wardroom.

Taking a deep breath I stand up determinedly, startling Nelson who's busy trying to make himself inconspicuous under the radiator. He wags his tail a little uncertainly – a reconciliatory gesture that I completely ignore (petty – who me?)

First things first – a liberal spray of my most expensive perfume focusing particularly on the armpits… (I know Nelson hates the smell – fitting punishment for getting me into this predicament.)

Secondly, a revamp of the make-up (using reading glasses to put on thus ensuring a seam free, ultra professional look – in a crisis like this I have no choice but to bring out the big guns…)

Ok, I'm ready.

I feel sick (but that could just be because I'm famished).

The Language School is quiet as I come out of the office and before I lose my nerve, I head down the stairs until I reach The Corridor. Then, taking a deep breath I begin walking nonchalantly towards the Wardroom, saying a casual 'hi' to everyone I pass (while waving my arm in the air at the same time to make certain that each person gets a blast of my perfume as they go by – this is no time for subtlety).

5 minutes later (not nearly long enough) I take a deep breath and push open the Wardroom doors.

It's now nearly 1 o'clock (ok 1300) so the bar is busy with people who've finished their lunch. I can see Sam – damn it, he's sitting with Rob. I just want a hole to swallow me up. This is the first time I've seen Rob this week.

I'm just about to leg it into the dining room when Rob looks over, sees me and waves. What the hell do I do now? Should I simply wave back and make a run for it – or is it better to hear the worst sooner rather than later...?

Would he have waved at all if he thought I had body odour issues?

I've hesitated too long and now have no choice but to face the music. Plucking up the courage, I walk over to their table with a casual 'hi guys'.

Rob looks up and smiles. "You smell nice," He says

"Bit better than this morning, hey Bev."

I completely freeze at Sam's comment and seriously consider simply throwing myself out the window to end the humiliation (even if the drop is only about 6 feet).
"Nelson was making some pretty horrendous smells when I saw you earlier – I was just telling Rob about it..."

He didn't think it was me.

Thank you, thank you, thank you God

I make a tolerable effort at a tinkling laugh and try to think of some witty response. "I know, he's terrible sometimes – but then of course he's a man." (I even manage a chuckle at this point – bloody hell I'm good.)

My parting shot? "Please don't tell the whole College will you; they might just think it was me..."

They both laugh. And just like that, the matter's dropped.

1345 I return to the office feeling lighter than air. Life is good again. I am back on track to becoming both superwoman and gorgeous babe of the year. (I resolutely ignore the voice inside asking me about the steak pie I had for lunch – it was simply an understandable emotional response to a narrow escape from complete disaster.)

Of course Nelson is pathetically grateful for my forgiveness which he shows by spending the rest of the afternoon sitting with his head in my lap.

He really does hate being in the doghouse.

1615 HRH duly returned to class this morning and he actually knocked on my door before leaving the language school for the day to ask (in English no less!) if he could give Nelson a biscuit. Ok so the request involved lots of hand waving and pointing, but I also distinctly heard the word 'give' and 'Nelson'.

And, it turns out he likes dogs – who'd have thought it?
Of course I said yes but encouraged him to drop the biscuit on the floor for Nelson to pick up – I was a bit concerned that if the greedy dog played his usual trick of lunging towards any outstretched hand, there would've been a definite risk of his royalness being off for the next month with an imagined case of

rabies.

Wednesday 23 September

1730 I've had a really interesting day today.

Firstly there was a meeting between the movers and shakers in the College (plus me) this morning. It seems that the Saudi Navy would like to send a small contingent of their Officer Cadets to be trained at BRNC. They will be needing English language training first so I just may actually have to go to Riyadh to discuss the possibilities with the head of the Saudi Navy (little old me – I can't quite believe it).

Of course I won't be going alone; Commander NTE will be accompanying me (although not sure how useful he'll be if some Sheikh wants to carry me off into the desert...)

I'm not quite convinced it's going to happen but, if it does, it's likely to be pretty soon as I've been told to make sure my passport is up to date and start the process for obtaining a Saudi Visa. I don't know whether to be thrilled or petrified.

Secondly, (definitely not ecstatic about this one) I've been asked if I want to take part in the Royal Marine Commando Challenge Charity event in 2 Saturdays time.

For those not in the know, the Commando Endurance Course is used by the toughest of the tough – the Royal Marines – to train their new recruits and once a year they allow members of the public to find out first hand exactly how it feels to get down and dirty, (but not in a good way) all for charity.

There are apparently obstacles with elegant names such as 'The Sheep Dip' and the Crocodile Pit.' I'm completely at a loss as to why some people might actually find this enjoyable. That said, I do feel under a certain amount of pressure in my new high profile role, (basically been told to get on and do it) so I've reluctantly agreed to be part of the team.

The blurb on the website is a bit off putting though...

"REMEMBER – this is a military fitness course and you should train like the Royal Marines do. During your training runs, drop and do press-ups, squats and crunches. This will prepare you for the frequent mid-race changes from running to crawling and back again. It's fair to say that on the cross country portion of the Challenge the maximum distance between obstacles can be as little as 500meters."

What the hell is a crunch...?

We have a resident Royal Marine based at the College who is going to put us through our paces - and, on the positive side, all this exercise means that I can quite legitimately forgo the rabbit food in favour of muscle building protein. If only I didn't have to run (and crawl) 4 kilometres at the end of it...

I hope Prince Charles appreciates all this effort.

Thursday 24 September

0830 Think I'm dying...

Came into work at 0730 this morning to take part in the first Commando training session.

On the plus side I now know exactly what a crunch is and am intimately acquainted with the muscles used to execute one.

On the minus side I'll be lucky if I'm actually walking again by the time we are supposed to be doing the bloody course.

Whose frigging idea was this?

1030 I'm completely starving and coffee and biscuits in the Wardroom are calling (I gave my own stash away to Nelson in the interests of reducing temptation...)

Unfortunately, as predicted, the backs of my calves feel like they've just been given a 20 minute stint on the rack, so it could take me a while to get there. But then perseverance is my middle name (especially when there's a biscuit at the end of it...)

Never let it be said that I have no strength of mind.

1040 It's taken me nearly 10 minutes to get down the stairs. As I round the last bend, the noise on the Quarterdeck alerts me to the fact that it's Shareholders – how could I have forgotten? (This is what too much exercise does for you...)

I hobble over to join the queue for coffee and unobtrusively look around to see if Rob's here (I can do inconspicuous when necessary).

We're now in to Week 3 and I've got no further forward in persuading him to ditch his bimbo girlfriend in the interests of a more mature, worldly wise sex machine on legs (aka me – or rather me when I'm not hobbling around like a 90 year old).

Come to think of it, I still don't know how old he is. I'm beginning to think it's time to toss subtlety aside.

1045 I finally have my coffee and can see Rob standing chatting to the 1st Lieutenant. Unfortunately he's over the other side of the room and the Commander is about to start his weekly College news update. Still, resourcefulness is my middle name (after perseverance).

I sidle slowly (and carefully of course – if I fall over today I think they may well have to stretcher me off) around the various groups while all the time trying to look as if I'm hanging on the Commander's every word and be inconspicuous at the same time (no easy feat, I can tell you).

Suddenly, unbelievably, I hear the Commander say my name and every eye in the room is centred on me expectantly...

Problem is, I might have *looked* as though I was hanging on every word, but sadly I haven't got a clue what he was on about.

I now understand just how a rabbit must feel when it's trapped in oncoming headlights.

I stand completely mute (it's not often I'm lost for words) frantically trying to think of something to say.

Luckily the person I'm standing next to takes pity on me and repeats the Commander's question in a low voice.
He simply wants to know how many are taking part in the Commando Challenge.

Breathing a sigh of relief, I lose my hunted expression and pass on that there are currently 5 of us – but of course we could always do with more recruits... There's a light sprinkling of laughter, the underlying tone of which is 'You must be bloody joking.'

The Commander finishes by advising people to come and see me if they're interested in taking part (no idea why he thinks they should come and see me – I'm the last person who knows what's going on...)

Still, it means that I have to stay where I am – just in case. I have no choice but to abandon my attempts to corner Rob and force him to confessing undying love (or at least get him to ask me up to his office for a coffee).

I don't anticipate a stampede of volunteers – some people actually have a choice of whether they risk life and limb to make a complete tit of themselves.

1105 I will definitely be buying the Commander a drink at the next Happy Hour. Turns out his announcement did me a huge favour.

Rob actually came over to tell me how impressed he was with my 'go getting' attitude and that although he would be unable to take part due to spending the weekend with his son, he'd be more than willing to support me in any way he can (I can think of a few ways off the top of my head but didn't think it appropriate to mention them in front of polite company...)

End result – we swap mobile phone numbers.

Definitely a sign.

He did sort of indicate that he expected to walk off the Quarterdeck with me. However, due to the fact that I'd been standing in one spot for the last 10 minutes, my legs had seized up all together and I was unable to move.

I couldn't reveal this of course, not while he was under the impression I'm a lean mean running machine! So I waved him on with the excuse that I really should wait to see if there are any more prospective idiots (sorry challengers) who wanted to sign up. Of course, once his back was turned, I frantically attempted to get my lower limbs working again by lifting alternate feet of the floor (while avoiding any life threatening hopping movement).

Then I limped slowly back to the Language School.

1715 Have spent the rest of the day holed up in my office working out timetables and catching up on emails. Luckily it's been raining for most of it so I don't feel so bad not taking Nelson for a walk. Have now got to somehow get myself to the car – should be ok as long as I take it slowly. For once Nelson's endless stopping, sniffing and peeing will work to my advantage – providing he doesn't start the ritual while we're walking down The Corridor. (Think I'll go the back way again just in case.)

2000 Frankie offers to give me a massage providing I wash my feet first and then cover the offending digits with 2 pairs of clean socks.

However, as tempting as the thought of my youngest daughter pummeling at my lower extremities is, (not) I decide to opt for a long hot bath instead with the aim of giving my aggrieved muscles a good soaking. The last time they were forced to perform like this was in 1985 when I was coerced into taking part in the parents' 3 legged race at Rosie's school sports day – my ex-husband is 6ft2.

2130 Beginning to get seriously concerned that I may actually have to wear flatties tomorrow if there is no improvement – thighs now starting to hurt as well...

Does this mean I can get out of training in the morning?

Friday 25 September

O800 Apparently not. Was ordered to jog on the spot for 20 minutes to loosen the muscles and improve my circulation. Now sitting in my office with the requisite bottle of water, feeling hot, sweaty and pissed off – mainly because my legs are actually feeling much better and I'm stuck for the rest of the day wearing (can hardly bring myself to say it) flat pumps...

Since when have I allowed common sense to get the better of me – why oh why didn't I bring a pair of heels as back up just in case.

I look like a munchkin in flat shoes – I've had to forgo wearing my customary suit and opt for the more casual skirt and sweater rig (you know the outdoorsy look complete with scarf and thick tights). Problem is, this get-up is fantastic if you're 6 feet tall with a figure that resembles a twig.

However, it doesn't look quite as eye catching (well not for the right reasons anyway) if you're 5 feet nothing with boobs that rival Katie Price in her Jordan days!
I sigh. Why should I be surprised after the week I've had.

Still, at least we've had no cadets fall asleep in class – must have made a lasting impression on the little darlings last week. (Have to say I'm pretty damn good at being an authority figure.)

1230 Spoke too soon. 2 students fell asleep in Caroline's class. She made the error of dimming the lights while playing a DVD –

fatal mistake.

Have decided to forgo lunch in the Wardroom and go the whole 'outdoorsy' hog by taking Nelson for a walk. Don't even have to change into trainers; just throw a poncho over the whole ensemble.

From a distance (about 400 metres...) I could be mistaken for a model out of Country Living magazine...

Keep my head down though just in case I bump into someone I know.

1315 Just got back in to the office to find a text from Rob asking me why I missed lunch – woo hoo.

Decide not to answer straight away – don't want to appear too eager...

1325 The 2 students who fell asleep are now waiting outside my office for their sentence. I decide to give them some additional duties over the weekend (can't really give them extra homework as this is theoretically giving the unfortunate impression that homework is a punishment – like we didn't understand that at school...?)

To give myself a little more time to devise something cunningly brilliant, I tell them to return to my office after class.

1450 Have so far failed to come up with anything remotely likely to dissuade them from falling asleep in class again so decide to go into the ILO to conspire with John – he's ex navy so should be able to come up with something suitably unpleasant.

1610 It's official. I really am now the most unpopular person in the language school (and possibly the world).
Throughout the weekend the 2 unfortunates will have to report hourly to the Commander who is providentially (of course he might not regard it in quite the same way) in the College both Saturday and Sunday.

Every time they knock on his door, he will give them something else to do...

Of course this won't continue throughout the night, they'll be able to stop after dinner.

Brilliant isn't it – what on earth would I do without John?

1645 We haven't had chance for a staff meeting this week, so we decide (in the interests of informality and a spot of team bonding) to do it down in the Royal Castle.

I still haven't responded to Rob's text and he's no doubt now left the site to zoom off to his girlfriend. I haven't *forgotten* to send it however (duh) This is all part of my clever strategy to make him think of me while he's with *her*. I just have to decide what to say and when the best time to send it is (in other words when is it going to be most awkward...)

It will definitely while away the three quarters of an hour I'm in the ferry queue.

1700 My glass of wine is going down far too well. Need to pace myself a bit – I can't have another because I'm driving.

It's no good; I'll just have to have some chips...

We order a bowl between us (that way we can hang on to our delusions), and get down to the nitty gritty.

How are we doing so far in the student development stakes...?

All 8 Kuwait Navy and 13 of the Kuwait Coastguard will very likely breeze through (they pay attention in class; actually do their homework *and* hand it in).

The remaining 2 Kuwait Coastguard and 4 of the Qatar Coastguard stand a pretty good chance of reaching the required language level (they mostly pay attention in class and *eventually* do their homework and hand it in).

6 of the Qatar Coastguard are unlikely to achieve the required level unless someone puts a proverbial rocket up their nether regions (i.e. me).

1 undercover royal who isn't showing any evidence that he'll get past "Big Mac please," at any time in the near future.

I can feel another cosy chat with Commander NTE coming.

1830 Am in the ferry queue and ready to create a masterful text in terms of both witty and cool.

First Draft...

Hi Rob sorry missed u at lunch but decided to do a 10 mile run instead...

1840 Second Draft:

Hi Rob sorry missed u at lunch- had a really busy day today...

1855 Third Draft:

Hi Rob...

Bloody hell, it's never taken me this long to write a text. What am I supposed to say anyway?

I need to be amusing yet empathetic; casual yet caring...

It's never taken me this long to write a student report.
And I'm now running out of time – definitely going to be on the next ferry so beginning to panic a bit.

Maybe I should leave it until I'm home and can get Frankie's input (hopefully without the smut).

1935 Arrive back at the flat and, on the positive side, Frankie's at home with her boyfriend James (who's a hairdresser so very useful at times like this, being very in touch with his feminine side..)

Unfortunately he's in the process of colouring Frankie's hair so there is hair dye all over the kitchen table and her recently sheared split ends all over the floor (which Nelson promptly decides to roll in before making himself comfortable on the living room sofa).

I pour each of us a glass of wine and park myself amid the debris to discuss the problem.

James suggests a raunchy response (maybe he's not quite as in touch with his feminine side as I thought...)

Frankie favours the more offhand, laid back approach (which takes bloody ages to compose).

45 minutes and 2 glasses of wine later, we come up with...

Hi Rob, didn't make lunch due 2 ongoing crunching commitments (slightly witty but shows I'm committed – hope *he* knows what a crunch is...)

Think about me on the beach this wkend, (conjuring up visions of me in a bikini rather than trainers and tracki bottoms).

as planning 2 do couple of 4k practice runs. (To the pub and back).

What r you up 2 this wkend? (So I'll know whether he's actually with his girlfriend or not, plus it might open up possible opportunities to flirt).

X (Really agonised over this but both Frankie and James agreed that he needs a push in the right direction...)

Think I need another drink.

Saturday 26 September

O800 Decide to have tea and toast in bed – with butter. Feeling very depressed. I didn't hear anything from Rob last night. Just knew I shouldn't have asked him a question, or ended the text with a kiss. He probably thinks I'm a desperate middle aged woman...

Plus really *have* got to do a run along the beach to practice for next Saturday – can't give my legs chance to go back on strike.

1200 Rosie, Frankie and James have agreed to meet me at the Boathouse. They're taking the car *and* Nelson in the interests of allowing me free rein to sprint some of the way should I feel the urge...

And they'll have a large glass of rosé ready and waiting for me.

1230 I finally arrive gasping and wheezing. All four of them (including Nelson) are looking at me with grins on their faces.

I refuse to rise to the bait and gathering my dignity, simply sit down and help myself to a large swallow of wine (medicinal).

Truth is, I'm too knackered to talk. Really beginning to get a little worried about my ability to rise to the challenge so to speak.

We order from the bar and, in my depressed (nobody's ever going to want me) state, I opt for scampi and chips with the justification that I might as well be fat as well as lonely, but also (on the off chance that the loneliness bit might be temporary) with the understanding that I fully intend to run back as well.

Unfortunately my offspring (plus James) are getting a bit fed up with my self-pitying mood so are not remotely interested in hearing my "Why oh why hasn't he texted me back?"

Also unfortunately, they are all so taken with giving me a lecture concerning zipping up man suits and growing some balls, that none of us are actually taking any notice of Nelson.

And again unfortunately, the lady on the next table is having a very passionate conversation with her partner involving much hand waving and gesticulating.

But most unfortunate of all, she has a large burger in the hand she's waving about which unbeknown to us, Nelson is eying with great interest.

Unintentionally, she thrusts the burger right under Nelson's nose who consequently proceeds to take a big bite out of it!

For a couple of seconds both our tables are actually speechless with disbelief while Nelson chews and swallows his prize with complete relish and much smacking of lips.

This rivals the poo incident in the embarrassment stakes.

I can't believe he's done this to me *twice* in one week...

Suddenly, everyone starts talking at once. I apologise profusely and immediately offer to buy her another burger.

Nelson is shoved under the table in disgrace with Frankie's foot on his head.

Luckily the couple are extremely understanding – it turns out they love dogs (even greedy and disobedient ones). The incident also put a stop to their argument – who knows, Nelson might even have saved their relationship...

He ended up having the rest of the burger (as punishment...)

2300 Still no text. I've spent the night in my bedroom doing the whole 'I want to be alone' thing.

My uncaring children have spent the night completely ignoring my moping and watching 'The X Factor'.

They didn't even bring me any chocolate.

I'm so unloved...

Sunday September 27

1200 In the interests of providing some variety in my running routine (and because I'm too embarrassed to go back to the Boathouse after yesterday) Jackie and I decide to meet for lunch at the other end of the beach at a pub called 'The Inn On The Quay' (This is a seaside town so we've got lots of choice...)

I relate the events leading up to the weekend expecting a little sympathy but unfortunately Jackie is of a similar opinion that 'desperation' is very unattractive in a professional woman of the world (I *think* she was talking about me).

She tells me in no uncertain terms (i.e. forcefully) that I am a very attractive woman in her prime of life who really does not need a man to make her happy...

And guess what? She's right.

I've survived quite well on my own since my divorce and, for the most part, I've actually been pretty content. I have an amazing job, wonderful friends and incredible (if unsympathetic) children.

This brooding is just not me.

Maybe Rob is, or maybe he isn't Mr Right, but whichever, I'm determined that from this moment on, I'm not going to agonize over it and allow it to dominate my every waking moment...

I feel like standing up and breaking into a rousing chorus of 'I Am Woman'.

Instead we order a bottle of wine (definitely easier on the ear) and talk about Prince Charles forthcoming visit to the College and what I'm going to wear to meet him...

You know what? My life really is actually pretty damn good...

Week 4

Monday 28 September

O800 I've just got back from my first training session of the week. I can't even begin to describe the pain of getting out of bed at 6am this morning to get to the College at 7. Nelson looked at me as though I'd lost the plot (really beginning to think he might be right).

Still, mustn't lose sight of the objectives:

1. Looking like a gorgeous babe (ok maybe babe is stretching it a bit – I'll go for gorgeous sophisticated glamorous woman in her prime...) when I meet Prince Charles

2. Completing the Commando Challenge in 5 days time without having to be resuscitated on site.

Think I'll have a coffee before I start work and a slice of toast to go with it (I read somewhere that anything you eat within an hour of exercising is completely calorie free – might as well put in 2 slices.)

Just before heading to the language school kitchen I glance down at my mobile phone. There's a text message from Rob...

My heart lurches (it really does – I'm actually quite embarrassed after my declaration yesterday.)

I decide that he'll just have to wait (being an independent woman who doesn't need a man in her life). I am determined not to read it until I've had my coffee and toast...

0807 Result? I've now got indigestion.

I open the text, not sure what to expect...

Turns out Rob has finished with bimbo girlfriend. (I resist the idea of dancing round the room.)

He's now feeling pretty low (step in sophisticated glamorous woman in her prime to take his mind of it...)

He apologised for not texting me back and hopes I'll forgive him. AND HE ENDS IT WITH A KISS.

So, now need to play this very carefully...

Show sympathy and understanding to ensure that he knows what a caring sharing person I am...

...but not too much – don't want him to moping around and thus not taking advantage of the opportunity that's right in front of his nose.

I settle for a short text saying how sorry I am and if he needs someone to talk to, I'm more than happy to listen (I know, bit clichéd but couldn't think of anything else!)

1030 Time for Stand Easy. I've made an extra special effort to look good today and you know what? I think I've actually lost a couple of pounds...

I'm wearing a fitted black dress (don't you just love black?) with knee high stiletto boots (makes me feel powerful and in control – you know, the whole 'I Am Woman' thing). Need to walk a little slower than normal in my 'Elvira Queen of the Night' boots but that's ok, it just means I'll make a bit of an entrance...

1105 Only saw Rob from a distance but he smiled over and nodded his head (practically a date – did I mention I'm an optimist...?)

And (yet more excitement!) HMS Argyll is visiting Dartmouth this coming Thursday. There's to be a cocktail party on board and I'm on the attendance list – woo hoo. God I love working here...

1430 I've just been informed that the visit to Saudi is definitely going ahead. The letter of invitation will be winging its way to both me and Commander NTE by the end of the week and the visit is scheduled for early November – eek. Still, at least I won't have to worry about what clothes to pack – everything will be hidden inside the long black thingy I'll be wearing. (Think it's called an 'abaya')

1615 Rob just texted back to ask if I fancy popping up to his office tomorrow for a coffee – I will of course accept but definitely for coffee only (no French Fancies) – need to play it cool for a bit...

What on earth am I going to wear? Sometimes life's just so complicated.

2230 I can't actually get into bed because it's entirely covered in clothes.

Frankie has been completely indifferent to my wails of "I've got nothing to wear." No sympathy from mum either and Jackie simply laughed when told of my dilemma and informed me (a little heartlessly I thought) that my wardrobe resembles the inside of Dorothy Perkins! (I'm sure she only meant the one in Torquay...)

And to top it all, Nelson has just made himself comfortable on top of my best black suit leaving ginger dog hairs all over the jacket.

How did I end up with such an uncaring family.

Ok, there's no panic, I just need to sit and think for a while and the perfect outfit will come to me (it's not that I'm shallow you understand...)

Think a glass of wine will help with the decision!

2335 I'm finally in bed with my chosen ensemble hanging on the outside of the wardrobe. I've gone for my fitted grey suit which actually fits me perfectly (even done up) *and* shows off my curves...

Can't wait for tomorrow.

Tuesday 29 September

O800 I decided (in the interests of not being hot red and sweaty when I go for coffee with Rob of course) to miss this morning's exercise session. Of course I didn't tell the Royal Marine PTI exactly that when he phoned to find out what my excuses were. They went more along the lines of a possible sprained ankle. Unfortunately he's now booked me in with the College physio...

Not yet sure how I'm going to get out of that one.

Still I'm not going to dwell on the problem. Live for the moment as they say. And my moment calls for a ginger nut – a moment that Nelson roundly applauds.

1030 One last look in the mirror and I'm ready. I actually feel a bit nervous. This will be the first time we've really spoken together alone. What if we have nothing in common?

Well there's only one way to find out. I tell Nelson to be a good boy (which he acknowledges with a particularly loud snore) and head out of my office.

1115 Good news or bad news...?

Good news – we seemed to have loads in common – including the fact that we actually share the same birthday, 21 May.

Bad news – Our actual dates of birth are 10 years apart.

Bugger!

He doesn't *look* 10 years younger than me but that just might be the grey hair...

And to be fair, he didn't flinch when I reluctantly admitted the year I was born – I could see him doing the sums in his head though.

Plus he's got a boat (and we're not talking rubber dinghy here – more a bloody great 45 foot yacht).

He asked me if I sailed....

I said I'd like to learn (in the same way that I'd like to Climb Mount Everest...)

Anyway, yachts and age differences aside, he's going to the cocktail party on Thursday; who knows what might happen.

1715 Sitting in the ferry queue after spending the last 45 minutes with the physio. If my ankle wasn't sore this morning, it certainly is now – this is what happens when vanity gets the better of you.

Wednesday 30 September

O 630 We're only at the end of September and I can't believe it's already dark, wet and cold. Of course it could just be that I don't normally venture out into the College grounds quite so early in the morning – certainly not to run up and down 'Cardiac Hill' (as it's quaintly referred to by the cadets). To be fair not even the most short-sighted observer would have called my effort this morning a run; pretty much resembled a stagger – I think our Royal Marine might have given up on me.

1400 I've just had a call from a PTI to inform me that one of the Qatari Coastguard hasn't turned up for sports afternoon. I resisted the temptation to say "What, only one?" and send John over to his cabin to check he's not gone to bed - the cadet that is, not John...

1420 Our loafer's been found in the Sick Bay - always the third place we look, after their bed and the Naafi. The International Cadets seem to regard the waiting room in sick bay as an impromptu rest area, getting them out of whatever activity they don't want to participate in (there are a lot of those) in the guise of suffering from whatever illness is currently fashionable (could be anything from acute pneumonia to a brain tumour depending on which website they've been on recently).

He is now waiting outside my office for the obligatory ticking off. I'm really going to have to get more creative with my punishments.

Is it time to go home yet...?

Thursday 1 October

O800 I left Nelson at home this morning – Cocktail parties on board warships and Irish terriers definitely not a good mix! I'm staying on board so given Frankie the pleasure of him tonight.

Which means I'll have the luxury of a 2 foot lumpy mattress all to myself – lucky me.

I really wanted to get out of training this morning but decided at the last minute that martyrdom was a good idea on this occasion for 2 reasons:

1. I've only got one more day before possible very public humiliation.

2. I may well be encouraged to eat and drink more this evening than is appropriate for my daily allowance of calories. Plus I may be rendered incapable of undertaking the last training session tomorrow morning.

So, suffering concluded for today, I am now showered and ready to get the day over with and jump straight to the sins of the night (not really sure how much sinning I'll have the opportunity to do but I live in hope...)

Really hope we don't have any major problems today.

0930 First major problem. Another of the Qatari Coastguard has not turned up for class (have you noticed a disturbing pattern here...?) and after a thorough search of his cabin and his usual haunts (like I said, under the bed, in the Naafi, over at Sick Bay) it looks as though he's done a bunk.

I blackmail one of the other cadets into giving me his mobile phone number (we should have already had it on file but they change their mobiles with the weather...) and call the absconder using his friend's phone (devious or what) which of course cons him into answering.

I don't waste time; merely tell him if he's not in my office in the next 15 minutes, I will quite simply chain him to his desk.

Once the shock of hearing my voice wears off, the cadet earnestly informs me that he is on his way to my office as we speak.

0940 No sign of cadet.

0945 No sign of cadet.

0950 Still no cadet. He has now had enough time to have got to my office on his hands and knees.Something is definitely afoot...

Knowing that I've blown any chance of him answering his mobile phone to me again, I call his friend into my office and advise said friend to text our errant cadet and inform him that if he doesn't call my office phone in the next 5 minutes, not only will he be banned from ever leaving the college again (probably for the rest of his life) but also his friend will suffer the same punishment (based on the fact that I know his friend knows where he is but is refusing to let on...)

0955 My office phone rings and a breathless, totally contrite voice tells me a thousand apologies but that he is currently in Sick Bay with the flu.

Which of course I know he isn't...

There is a noise in the background – it sounds like a train whistle. "Are you on a train?" I ask incredulously

There's slight silence on the other end of the phone as the culprit tries desperately to think of a way out (his English really is not *that* good).

In the end he offers another thousand apologies and informs me that he has been called to London to meet with his grandfather who is over from Qatar for the weekend. "Ma'am," He continues solemnly, "you must understand, I cannot go against the wishes of my grandfather."

Now the usual route for International Cadets to apply for additional leave is through their Embassy, but I know for certain we've had no such request from Rashid at the Qatar Embassy. I brusquely inform the cadet that I will be contacting his Military Attaché immediately to confirm the truth of his statement, to which there is a panicked "But ma'am," on the other end of the line before I ruthlessly cut the call and briskly tell John to contact the Qatar Embassy.

1005 The Embassy has confirmed that not only is our cadet's grandfather not in the country but that he has been dead for the last 10 years.

My subsequent text goes something like this:

Your embassy says that your grandfather is now with Allah so unlikely to be in London at the same time. I will expect you in my office first thing tomorrow morning. YOUR FATHER WILL BE INFORMED

That should do it. Time for Shareholders…

1725 I thought the day was never going to end. Freely admit I've not really been with the program (although reliably informed that our missing cadet is on his way back – I'll reserve judgement for tomorrow morning).

I'm really looking forward to this evening. I give Sarah a quick call (of course she's going) and grab my overnight bag before heading up to my cabin.

Everyone's meeting in the Wardroom for pre-party drinks at 1815 so I really need to get my skates on.

I'm planning to wear trousers this evening as my experience of previous cocktail parties on warships has taught me a couple of dos and don'ts – for example...
Trousers are a must if you don't want every Tom Dick and Harry sticking his head up your skirt as you negotiate treacherous ladders to get on to the ship.

Start off with sexy top but NEVER come without thermal back up – It's usually bloody freezing on the deck (even in the summer).Thus, my top is black and clingy – and so is my vest underneath. On my bottom half, black wide leg evening trousers and heels (can't possibly go in flatties – I'll just have to manage and I *have* done this before). I've also got a nice black wool evening wrap – not quite cold enough for my faux fur.

1810 I'm all ready. Yep I've definitely lost some weight – didn't have to lie on the bed to get the trousers done up – plus they're not giving me a wedgie (Just in case you don't know what a wedgie is, Wikipedia's definition is as follows: 'A wedgie occurs when a person's underwear or other garments are wedged between the buttocks.')

And we all know it's a *very* unattractive look...

1825 Sarah and I arrive in the Wardroom to find everyone already making inroads into the gin and tonics ready prepared on the bar. The mini buses are leaving for the jetty in just over 5 minutes which means we've definitely got time for one...

1840 We arrive at the jetty to find a couple of motor whalers waiting for us and 5 minutes later we're heading towards the huge grey warship moored in the middle of the river.

1900 It's taken nearly 20 minutes to get the whole party on board and I'm now standing happily with full glass of champagne in one hand and a plate of canapés in the other.

I must remember not to overindulge this evening...

I *must* remember *not* to overindulge this evening...

1930   Already on second glass of champagne and really beginning to enjoy myself. I haven't had chance to chat with Rob yet but then he'll have to join the queue.

One of the nicest things about being a single woman at a naval cocktail party is that there aren't many of us; consequently we're in high demand to provide sparkling and witty conversation...

At the moment I'm surrounded by a small crowd of junior officers who are always great company (being not quite so up themselves as some of their older counterparts). The downside to their enthusiasm is their eagerness to keep my glass filled up.

"Can I get you another drink ma'am?" Is coming from all directions and in short order the canapés have been whisked away and each hand is now holding an alcoholic beverage.

I must remember not to overindulge this evening...

The trouble is I'm beginning to forget why I mustn't overindulge this evening.

All of a sudden the junior officers melt away and after wondering for a second if I'd said something unfortunate (you know like I'm feeling a bit pre-menstrual at the moment) I'm suddenly faced with the broad (in the sense of corpulent) chest of the ship's Commanding Officer.

My eyes travel upwards in the hope that the head on the top of the rotund torso inches away from my nose is an improvement.

It's not. And what's more, it's leering at me in a very un-officer like manner (more of a smirk really).

My heart sinks and I instantly begin to sober up. I glance around frantically looking for a way out but everyone is occupied and aside from a couple of sympathetic glances, I am being roundly ignored by everyone thinking to themselves "Thank God it's not me..."

Berating myself for being so unkind, I take a deep breath to introduce myself politely. However, before I can open my mouth a large fleshy finger comes up to chuck me under the chin before saying, "What pretty little morsel do we have here then?"

My mouth snaps shut as I stare up at the dinosaur in front of me.

Nobody told me that the ship's Captain was a knob – why didn't anybody tell me?

And why didn't anybody tell the idiot that this kind of behaviour went out with press gangs and scurvy!

Having no other choice I smile up at him while taking a step backwards to put a little space between us.

Which he immediately steps into...

I'm beginning to feel a bit panicky – there are only another couple of paces back to the ship's railings. If I'm not careful I'll end up overboard (a bit like being made to walk the plank).

Completely oblivious to my discomfort, my tormentor actually winks at me and all of a sudden I'm actually fighting the urge to jump overboard voluntarily...

Then my knight in shining armour (or in this case mess undress) comes to the rescue in the form of Rob, trailed unenthusiastically by one of my earlier admirers who looks as if he'd rather be anywhere but here.

Without ceremony Rob politely asks if he can speak with the Captain for a moment; then he turns to me and asks if I'll excuse them both, before directing the cadet to escort me to the bar.

I fight the urge to kiss him (Rob that is, not the Captain) and hurry after my reluctant cadet who's already beating a hasty retreat.

Phew, that was a close call.

Must remember to thank Rob later...

I spend the rest of the evening avoiding the Captain who luckily decides he has bigger fish to fry (in every sense of the word) in the form of Lt Commander Kate Donohue who appears to be hanging on his every word (not to mention his cummerbund which incidentally has slid down off his waist to very near the top of his trousers!)

I don't think I can look anymore...

2100 Time to go. Unfortunately the wind's gotten up during the evening and I'm seriously worried that I won't be able to climb in to the waiting motor whaler. (I'd probably have been even more scared if I'd been sober and actually able to see how much it was rocking.)

However, just as I'm unsteadily trying to find the bottom of the boat with my flailing left foot (and nearly braining a few people in the process!) a pair of warm hands come around my waist and expertly lift me off the ladder and into the waiting vessel.

My scream is cut off just before it erupts as I find my rescuer is none other than Rob, coming to my aid for the second time (my hero). With his hands still on my waist, he grins at me and I go all gooey inside...

...I can't remember the last time that happened.

Then he unceremoniously deposits me onto a bench before helping down the next person (definitely not as intimately as he did me – though that could have been because it was the Commodore's wife).

Sarah plonks herself next to me to let me know that the party is continuing up at the Wardroom and asks if I'm coming. I nod my head enthusiastically and try to ignore the little voice in my head telling me that I really should be heading to bed for some reason or another...

2330 4 more gin and tonics later and I know I've had enough. The voice in my head is now using a loudspeaker to get my attention and the room is seriously beginning to spin.

Think I'd better quit while I'm ahead (even if only slightly...)

Friday 2 October

O800 Why isn't there a lock on my office door so I can die in peace?

I have vague memories of flirting with Rob (completely without any subtlety unfortunately). My only hope is that he was as trollied as I was and so doesn't remember my embarrassing indiscretions. Apart from one that is...

My mind is taken briefly off my wish for a peaceful demise as I recall the conclusion to the evening - even if it is a little blurred around the edges.

I remember making my excuses to all and sundry and then (as if by magic...) suddenly finding Rob at my side as I walked (or rather weaved my way) along the Corridor to my cabin.

Taking my arm, he informed me with a smile that he wanted to make sure I arrived at my destination safely (not sure if he meant minus a broken ankle or without any undue interference from other inebriated parties).

Still who cared? We arrived at my cabin far too quickly and I was soo tempted to invite him in for a night cap (despite the fact that I hadn't got any alcohol in my room).

However, before I could say anything, he bent his head and kissed me briefly on the lips. Then, after wishing me good luck for Saturday, he turned on his heel and left...

Does a kiss mean he likes me? I ponder for a second before realising that my head is in no fit state to join in my usual dissecting session.

I'll think about it later if I survive that long.

0835 I've just finishing interviewing our runaway cadet who arrived back in the college late last night. To put it mildly, he's not a happy bunny.

He has apparently been hauled over the coals by his Embassy which he thought extremely unfair given the circumstances – the *real* circumstances – which he took great pains (and an inordinate length of time – did I say I wasn't feeling well?) to earnestly explain to me.

It seems that his disappearance from the College (although obviously not to visit his dead grandfather) was, at the end of the day, driven by a completely altruistic motive! It appears that he has a friend who is studying in London and who's gotten himself into serious financial difficulties (in itself pretty farfetched given that he's from Qatar and can afford to study in the UK and London to boot) but, apparently this friend had saved up the money himself. He is also evidently very proud, and (this was the crux of the matter) had refused to accept a gift of money wired to him electronically.

Now, I have to say our fugitive's continued sincerity was beginning to win me over (and I really wanted a lie down) so I tried butting in (you know – don't worry about it, we'll put it behind us, you won't get 100 lashes, that sort of thing...)

But his next words took to wind out of my sails really...

"I had to make sure he was OK ma'am – you see the problem is, my friend believes I know f*ck nothing about being without money."
I blinked at this revelation and was about to berate him for

using the 'f' word to someone who's essentially his commanding officer (that's me...) but then he went on to say with even more passion...

"But he's wrong ma'am, he's wrong. I'm sure *you* will believe me when I say I know f*ck all"

Yep, that about sums it up!

I just didn't have the heart (or the energy) to either berate him or correct him, so I let him go with the usual punishment of a weekend remaining on board. I know it's not really much of a punishment as he'd only just got back from London, but I'm *really* not feeling well.

1030 Decide against Stand Easy – don't think it's a good idea to leave my office, at least until the shaking's stopped.

1230 Decide against lunch – don't think it's a good idea to leave my office, at least until the cold sweats have stopped...

1415 I'm forced to leave the office due to the fact that I need another passport photograph to send to the Saudi Embassy in support of my Visa application. Unfortunately in the resulting picture, I look like a 7 day old corpse that's been dug up!

And, even more unfortunately, it has to go off today.

Oh well, at least the real me will be an improvement on the photo (not likely to be hung-over in Riyadh).

1600 Have spent the rest of the afternoon holed up in my office until I can legitimately go home (in other words until I'm under the legal limit).

Which is now...

2100 I'm only just beginning to feel human again – really beginning to worry that my overindulgence may have an effect on my performance in the Challenge tomorrow...

Saturday 3 October

O700 It's raining.

0800 It's still raining.

0900 Just leaving for Lympstone and the Commando Challenge – it's *still* raining.

What are the chances of me drowning on this assault course? If so, my boots are very likely to play a large part in my demise – visions of me sinking to the bottom of 10 foot deep flooded pond never to be seen again are beginning to haunt me.

I get no sympathy from my offspring who decide that I look hilarious in my combat gear (they did begrudgingly sponsor me though I don't know why I bothered, I'll only have to give them the money back later...)

However, I am able to ignore their less than respectful hoots of laughter as I've received a text of support and encouragement from Rob. I decide to get back to him later (if I'm not in hospital).

Our nominated starting time is 1100 which means we have to register by 1000 – we'll apparently have a briefing, then be taken (in a military truck...) to the course start for a 10 minute warm up (what makes them think 10 minutes will be enough...?)

At least we're not insane and doing the 10km challenge (which involves a 3km run either side of the obstacle course – puleease!)

There are 6 of us all together: 2 lecturers from the Navigation Department (not sure how easy it is to get lost on this course); 1 lecturer of strategic studies (I don't think Naval history is likely to help any, but you never know); the College Chaplain (in case we need to pray) and, (our ace in the hole) a PTI.

Then of course there's me – I like to think of myself as the team's wild card! (Or, more accurately, the idiot who stepped in at the last minute...)

The PTI is the only other female in our team, but that's where the similarity ends as she's about 6 foot tall, does a passable imitation as an Amazon Warrior and looks like she should be doing mud wrestling in her spare time (which would stand her in very good stead for today).

Our Royal Marine training instructor is driving us there in the College mini bus. He can't take part, but he's coming along to give us moral support, (or possibly have a good laugh...)

1035 Our brief has just finished – what the hell am I doing here...?????

No time to back out now, we're being herded on to the truck to be taken to the start of the obstacle course. (I need a leg up to get in – not a good start really, hope it's not a forerunner of things to come.) I'm feeling really sick, but that could just be the bacon sandwich I had when we arrived.

1045 We arrive at the start of the obstacle course. The 1st thing I notice are the hoards of spectators (nothing like making a tit of yourself in public). The 2nd thing is the very yummy Royal Marine doctor standing near to the starting line. Suddenly the prospect of resuscitation doesn't seem so daunting – he can put me in the recovery position any time!

My imaginings are rudely interrupted by Paula (did I mention that our PTI is the leader of our little band) and we begin our warm up.

10 minutes later I'm already sweaty, knackered and want nothing more than to throw myself at the feet of the gorgeous doctor and beg him to take me away from all this...

No such luck.

1055 We take our place in the queue of idiots (sorry participants) waiting to start, and our trusty leader takes us through a couple of last minute instructions. I resist the urge to make eye contact with said gorgeous doctor because I don't want him to see me trailing behind the rest of my team.

Then we're off...

Is it a bit late to consider the fact that I'm claustrophobic, swim like a brick and really really hate the idea of being underwater...?

Still, at least it's stopped raining.

The first part of the course isn't too bad. A nice track, newly clear blue skies and the sun is making it actually quite pleasant – feels like I'm out on a jaunt with Nelson. I'm beginning to wonder what all the fuss is about.

Then the track turns and starts leading us down hill and we start to get wetter and wetter...

We get to the bottom of the hill and another really nice helpful Marine tells us to lay face down in some thick gloopy mud and crawl on our bellies through it into a nearby stream.

Do they have leeches in England? God I think I might have kissed a worm.

It's bloody freezing.

What am I *doing* here...?

Next up a waist deep stream (for most people, for me it was more like chest deep) and into the 'Crocodile Pit'

I can't feel my feet anymore. How long does it take to get foot rot?

Paula yanks me out of the Dip (is it my imagination or does she seem to be pulling a little harder than necessary...?)

Next up we tackle the 'Track Wade'. Another mud bath but this time it's serious. I can hardly force one foot in front of the other...

What am I doing here?

Once out of the Track Wade, we jog (yeah right...) along a short track to what the Marine's jokingly call 'The Smartie Tube'.

I stand staring at the two underground sewer pipes half full of water

Did I say I suffer from claustrophobia?

I'm not sure I can do this.

The last of my team mates disappears into the black maw as I hesitate. Then fear of being left behind (plus the comment of 'get a move on Shorty' coming from the queue developing behind me) releases me from my immobility (did I say I suffer from claustrophobia?)
Then I'm crawling through inky blackness, pulling myself along by my arms.

I can't see a thing and 10 metres in the muscles in my arms decide to go on strike. I have a bright idea to turn on my back thinking that I can always wriggle out backwards...

Not a good idea (as I realize very quickly that I can't move at all) especially when someone crawling up behind me touches my ankle – hope my resulting boot in the head doesn't give him a concussion.

Think I could well be having 'coffin dreams' for the rest of my life.

I exit the tube just as I'm beginning to hyper ventilate, only to be pulled onwards again straight into a tunnel they call the 'Knee Crunch'.

And then onto another tunnel – they're beginning to blur now.

We must be near the end surely?

No such luck.

'Peter's Pool' comes next.

I don't know who the hell Peter is but if I did, he'd be crossed off my Christmas card list for starters.

More chest deep freezing cold water with a grinning photographer waiting at the other end.

I am now wet right down to my birthday suit, am approximately 30 pounds heavier than I was at the start and can definitely feel something wriggling down my back!

I'm being urged onwards by my intrepid team members and I resist the urge to commit physical violence (too knackered anyway). I am then dragged down the 'Steep Gully' and into *another* thigh deep boggy pond.

WHAT AM I DOING HERE?

Then it's the 'Sheep Dip'...

I stand in the queue waiting to negotiate through the *totally submerged underwater* sewer pipe

Did I say I'm claustrophobic?

It is absolutely no consolation that there is a Royal Marine at each end of the tunnel pushing and pulling hapless participants through what is essentially an underwater drain pipe.

What if I get stuck?

I'm rooted to the spot, lost in visions of myself drowning (in full colour with added stereo). I get as far as planning my funeral eulogy before being beckoned forward by an impatient Marine who pulls me into a crouch at the tunnel entrance. I feel like Marie Antoinette crouching before the guillotine.

I realise that the soldier is giving me a quick brief as to what to do and I can't help it, I pull back in panic. My breathless attempts to ask if I can go around it are met with an unsympathetic "You're going through."

I think the bastard's enjoying this.

Then he's counting down from 3 to give me a chance to take a (last) breath before he ruthlessly pushes me under.

Oh my God, oh my God, oh my God I'm going to die.........

Then my collar is grabbed and I'm being dragged out the other side – right on cue for another official photographer.

I stagger to my feet, wiping the muddy water out of my eyes and blink up at my team mates who are standing at the edge of the Dip laughing.

I wonder how long a prison sentence I'd get for bumping off my 5 insensitive colleagues (horribly of course) and make an effort to clamber out of the pond.

Unfortunately my 'get up and go' has now completely 'got up and gone' and I'm shamefully forced to accept a helping hand from one of my soon to be horribly murdered team mates.

"Come on old girl," Trills Paula as she jogs off in the lead. "Only one more obstacle to go."

Old girl! I grit my teeth and stagger in the same direction while narrowing my imaginary fiendish scheme down to one person...

The last obstacle is known as the 'Black Bog', which, as its name implies, is full of thick black waist deep mud and peat. I wonder (slightly hysterically at this point I'm ashamed to say) whether the muck would provide a good face pack – just before finding out first hand as I trip and fall face down.

After what feels like an eternity I am unceremoniously yanked up to the accompaniment of a disgusting sucking sound...

I now resemble a yeti.

I splutter and spit out the revolting black goo while fighting the urge to cry.

That's it, I'm done. My callous, cold hearted team mates will just have to leave me here to rot away slowly and painfully starting with my extremities... (Thank God I never had my nails done.)

Suddenly, without warning Paula bends forward and heaves me out of the mud and throws me roughly over her right shoulder. Wading forward, she carries me almost effortlessly (I must have lost weight) to the edge of the bog and plonks me unceremoniously into the hands of my surprisingly sympathetic team mates...

The final jog (or rather lurch on my part) to the finish line is a bit of a blur and I feel like I've just survived an episode of 'I'm a Celebrity Get Me Out of Here'...

Then it's a team photo (not sure how I can avoid this one going into the Britannia Magazine...) and then back on the army truck to the *best* part of the day...

...a hot shower followed by a fortifying glass of wine.

Would I do it again?

Err, not a chance...!

Sunday 4 October

O900 Frankie has actually brought me tea and toast in bed – think she might have been a little worried last night when I got back – especially as she had to practically carry me up the stairs to the flat (to be fair, that might have been partly due to the 4th glass of wine I had in celebration – not that I have any intention of telling her; determined to milk this for all it's worth).

0910 Just tried to get out of bed to go the toilet and had to resort to crawling on my hands and knees. Maybe it wasn't the alcohol after all.

Think I'll just stay in bed for the rest of the day with Nelson.

I go over yesterday in my mind and somehow it doesn't seem so horrific anymore (apart from possible permanent muscle damage and two broken nails).

I'm actually quite proud of myself – at least I got to the finishing line without needing mouth to mouth.

I spend some time planning how I can avoid our team photo going into the College magazine. My text to Rob last night was a little sketchy on the truth...

Result: He still thinks I'm a bit of a fitness buff.

Think it might be better to let him down gently – he needs to get to know me a bit first...!

Week 6

Monday 12 October

1 015 I can't believe it's been over a week since I completed the Commando Challenge and I'm only now losing the John Wayne walk...

Last week was pretty much a write off really apart from basking in the admiration of my colleagues who didn't have the courageous spirit (ok, who weren't pressured) to take on such a challenge.

Of course the pictures haven't been made public yet.

I haven't seen Rob for over a week – just when it seemed that things were hotting up between us. Apparently he's away doing something with submarines. (Only just found out he's a submariner which was a bit of a blow because I've always been told that hygiene is an afterthought with most of them. Ok so I haven't got *that* up close and personal but not noticed any smelly armpits so I'm giving him the benefit of the doubt...)

Anyway, it's probably a good thing that I haven't been otherwise distracted because this week I have to concentrate on THE ROYAL VISIT – woo hoo!

Prince Charles is coming on Thursday and the College has been in a fever of anticipation for the last week. We've not been given the timetable of his visit yet but I've been told that I'm still on for a meeting...

Just one *small* problem though, apparently the PTB (Powers That

Be) think it would be a good idea if I take along a few of the Internationals to give the Prince a taste of the RN's contribution towards the UK's Defence Diplomacy.

Now in theory this is a good idea (apart from the fact that it will of course scotch any chance I have of flirting with the current fourth in line to the throne – not that I'm shallow as you know).

The problem is that given his connections (despite the fact that we're still not supposed to be aware of them) our resident HRH will obviously expect to be one of the chosen few and although we are now in Week 6, he has so far shown no further improvement since pointing at Nelson and saying "dog" with an enormous grin on his face.

Likeable he is bless him; fluent he still certainly is not and as such is not really a terribly good advertisement for our teaching skills...

Still, no sense in worrying until I'm forced to give out names (maybe I should just put them in a hat).

Think it's time for Stand Easy.

Now this is going to take even longer than usual because The Corridor has been polished to within an inch of its life in preparation for 'The Visit' (think they're banking on the fact that as Prince Charles was in the RN, he actually trained at BRNC so should be up to speed with the lethal nature of the flooring...)

Hopefully the number of casualties won't run into double figures.

1105 Have just to come back to the office to find that the PTB have moved International Day from this Wednesday to Thursday to tie in with The Visit.

International Day is held once a term on the Quarterdeck and it's generally a great opportunity for all the Internationals training at the College to show and talk about their respective countries and cultures.

The good news is that it means I won't have to nominate students to meet with the Prince. The bad news? Lots more opportunities for embarrassing faux pas (otherwise known as f*ck ups).

Still, not my problem. I'll call a meeting with the teachers after the lessons today so that we can discuss the contributions of the English Language students and nominate volunteers (yeah right).

1450 Just found out that the formal invitations to Saudi Arabia have arrived at the College. My visa's also come back (the photograph really is *bad*) I'm accompanying Commander NTE, and (wait for it...)

We're flying FIRST CLASS...

I can hardly contain my excitement. The nearest I've ever got to going first class anywhere was a free upgrade with British Rail (and the best that can be said about that was the fact that the dry sandwiches and luke warm coffee were free).

I resist the impulse to dance around the room and decide instead to treat myself and Nelson to a donut from the Naafi - will start the diet again tomorrow...

Life is GOOD.

1530 Scratch that. Life is *not* good. I've just been informed that they want me to do a speech on the Quarterdeck about the importance of International Training in Defence Diplomacy.

IN FRONT OF PRINCE CHARLES.

Bugger, bugger, bugger.

Why on earth do they want me to do it?

I've only got 2 days to put it together and the possibility of making a complete tit of myself in front of Royalty makes me feel sick.

Whose bloody idea was this...?

I wonder if there's any way out of it and decide to make a few frantic phone calls.

1600 Apparently there's not a cat in hells chance – the directive has come from the Commodore and for some reason he wants a civvie to make the speech (some viper definitely gave him the idea of me being the proverbial lamb to the slaughter though and when I find out who...)

1830 Already on my second glass of wine. I really need to get a grip. I've never spoken in front of Royalty before...

What am I going to say?

Oh God, what am I going to *wear*?

Tuesday 13 October

O815 I've been awake all night and now sitting at my desk with my pen poised over a completely empty piece of paper...

Nelson is staring at me expectantly – he knows my stressed out look generally results in something sweet coming his way.

Ok, where to start...

1035 Finally managed to put together an initial draft for my speech so not feeling quite so desperate. In fact I'm even starting to warm to the idea. It really is a good opportunity to blow the International cadets' trumpets to the British cadets who are not always particularly sympathetic to their mostly Middle Eastern oppos (I wonder how many of the British YOs could complete the RNYOC in Arabic).

Actually beginning to look forward to it...

1245 Don't know where the morning's gone. Decide to check my emails before I head down to the Wardroom for lunch. Despite the fact that there are already about 50, one from VSO jumps out at me. Yey, an email from Rob - he must be back at the College. And the subject line is 'Lunch?'

Expecting him to be simply checking whether I'm going down to the Wardroom today, I'm totally blindsided by his request to take me out for lunch tomorrow...!

Is this a date?

Impulsively I decide against going down to the Wardroom and take Nelson out for walk instead - in the interest of keeping him in suspense so to speak. (Rob that is, Nelson couldn't give a carrot who I eat with as long as *his* stomach is amply catered for). I'll answer the email when I get back – gives me time to decide whether to accept or not (who am I kidding?)

1400 Back sitting in front of the computer working out how to reply to Rob's email. As always, don't want to appear too eager but don't want to seem too stand offish either. Obviously in addition to really getting to know him, this is also an ideal opportunity to assess any potential BO issues without actually asking him outright. ("So, Rob, how often do you wash on average?" Not exactly an ideal subject for small talk…)

Bloody hell, this dating lark is hard work. Could really do with another donut to help bring out my wittiness and sparkle but I've already had my quota this week (trying very hard to hang on to the image of 'gorgeous sophisticated glamorous woman in her prime').

1421 20 minutes later and my imaginative yet deceptively simple reply is…

Sounds Good (Should really have succumbed to the donut!)

His response is gratifyingly quick leading me to the warming conclusion that he had been waiting with bated breath for my reply (or he was in the process of checking his emails).

Will pick you up in the car park at 1230 tomorrow if that suits. Know a lovely village pub a couple of miles away.
Rob x

And just like that, all worries about Royalty go completely out of my head…

It will of course necessitate an extra long lunch but that's not a problem as I'll just stay later tomorrow night and put the finishing touches to my admittedly short but nevertheless impassioned speech.

1715 We've managed to organise the International English Language cadets in their preparations for International Day. They have been told of the impending Royal Visit and the importance of putting on a good show. I just wish I could rid myself of this slightly nauseous feeling of impending doom...

An hour in the ferry queue ought to do it...

Wednesday 14 October

O915 Feel as though I've done a day's work already. I couldn't sleep last night – I'm actually a little nervous (it's not that long since I had a date – is it?) so decided to get up at 6 this morning to wash my hair etc. Got in to work at 0730 (already making up for extra extra long lunch – hopefully).

I'm wearing a black pencil skirt (new – bought it over the weekend) which fits me like a glove. I've teamed it with a black and white striped shirt (again fitted of course – *and* with no gaping boob gaps) which has touches of red at the collar and cuffs. Then I've finished the whole ensemble with red court shoes...

I've put my hair back in a French plait (sexy *and* business like).

God I look good – if he doesn't fancy me in this get up, he's gay!

I've gone over my speech a few times (while looking at myself in the mirror to make sure that I'm standing up straight and holding my stomach in just in case they take any photos).

I sound pretty good, definitely on a roll.

Today is going to be *awesome...*

1230 Oh. My. God.

He has a Lotus

A bloody *Lotus*!

I look down and part my legs experimentally – there is a *potential* gap of about 18 inches...

How the hell am I going to get in it?

I'm beginning to sweat as Rob drives up waving.

I plaster a smile on my face as I walk up to the passenger's side just as Rob leans over and opens the door. "Hop in," He says with a grin.

In fact he doesn't open the door. It's actually just a window. There is a ledge that I'm supposed to 'hop' over.

I stand helplessly for a second wondering if I should just tell him I'll drive myself.

"It's much easier if you slide in backwards." Comes Rob's accommodating response to my hesitation.

I want to hit him.

I look around to see if anybody's watching but for once (thank you God) the car park is deserted. Then throwing caution to the winds and my handbag into the foot well, I tentatively place my bottom onto the ledge and slide backwards.

Result? I'm stuck with my legs hanging out of the window and my head in Rob's lap.

I glare at his obvious enjoyment of the situation and resist the impulse to ask what a grown man is doing with a bright yellow dinky toy.

Using my hands to lever myself up and with Rob's help pushing my shoulders, I manage to swing my legs through the window and lever myself into a sitting position.

I am never *ever* going to be able to get out...

My face is now sweating profusely and I can practically feel my foundation starting to slide (think I'm going to have to invest in some tinted moisturiser for situations calling for a slightly lighter touch – like this one). Luckily my French plait has got so much hairspray in it that it doesn't move an inch!

Taking a couple of deep breaths, I buckle up the seat belt. I daren't look over at Rob in case I start crying.

First he goes out with a bimbo and next he has a ridiculous car.

I'm beginning to think it's not going to work out...

As Rob manoeuvres the car on to the main road, I take a few deep breaths and begin to relax a little; I'm even starting to feel a slight thrill at the feel of the powerful engine picking up speed (I'm obviously no more immune to fast cars than the next person – which is good because I might well be spending the rest of the day in it.)

Rob glances over at me. "I know, pretty impractical isn't it?" He says with a grin that makes him look 12 years old.

"Boys and their toys." I shrug and smile back, still trying to work out how I'm going to get out of the damn thing without sliding over the ledge head first.

"It was a present to me from me after the separation. Everything had been so shit and I needed something to make me feel good about myself again."

Now *that* I can identify with. I went a bit mad and had a tattoo after my divorce came through (mind you, it cost a bit less and I was restrained enough to have it where it can only be seen by a very select few...)

"And I just love driving it," He continues, "Makes me feel less of a crusty old submariner and of course my son Jack thinks it's cool.

"Not to mention the fact that it annoys the hell out of my ex-wife!"

I laugh, understanding all those reasons perfectly.

The mention of his main job in the RN reminds me of my secondary purpose in accepting Rob's luncheon date...

"Why did you become a submariner?" I ask, genuinely interested in why anyone would want to spend entire months in a big black tin can.

"My dad was in the Submarine Service and he took me on board when I was 11. Since then it's always been my ambition to drive a submarine."

I fight the urge to break into a rendition of 'Stingraaay, Stingray...' and nod sagely as though I understand perfectly. "What's it like being in one?" (I'm thinking this might lead to jokey comments about washing – sneaky or what...?"

Rob spends the rest of the drive regaling me with tales of life under the ocean wave but doesn't unfortunately mention hygiene (or more importantly lack of it), and all too soon we arrive at our destination – a small but quaint village pub called the Green Dragon.

As Rob expertly manoeuvres himself out of the driver's seat, my heart begins to thud in my chest. I have absolutely no idea how I'm going to get out. He opens the passenger door with a flourish and looks at me expectantly.

I look helplessly back. "Er, I'm not sure how to do this..." I really hate the way my voice comes out all helpless and whiney.

Rob advises me to lean back and lift my legs over the sill, then to give him my hands and he will pull me out (a bit like a cork out of a wine bottle). This would be ok except that I'm wearing hold ups which will give him a bird's eye view of my knickers.

I slide backwards on the seat and swing my legs round making an effort to keep them together (not that difficult given that my skirt is akin to wearing a large Smartie tube). As Rob bends forward to grab my hands, I resist the urge to kick him in the chin 'accidentally' with the tip of my stiletto (where did this propensity for violence come from...?)

A couple of seconds later he heaves me (thank God I've lost a few pounds!) through the window and I land on my feet with a resounding thump.

He's standing very close to me and his hands are still holding mine. My heart begins to thump for a slightly different reason and all of a sudden I don't care about bright yellow dinky toys. I breathe in the scent of him and it's all wholesome male with an undertone of delicious cologne.

Not a smelly armpit in sight.

He leans down and gently kisses me on the lips. I'm sure he meant to leave it at that but I've had enough pussy footing around – It's time to get this show on the road so to speak. So putting my arm around his neck, I hold his head down to mine and allow the kiss to deepen. He responds with satisfying enthusiasm; his mouth warm and firm. For a brief time we actually forget where we are (well Rob definitely does – it's left to me to gently disentangle myself and step back.)

I make an effort to act a little blasé about the encounter but my heart's beating ten to the dozen belying my outward calm. I feel like I'm 18 again – can't remember the last time I made out in a car park.

The pub is warm and cosy with a welcoming open fire even though it's not yet November. I seat myself in a secluded corner while Rob goes to the bar to order drinks and grab a menu.

There's a warm glow in the pit of my stomach that has nothing to do with the log fire.

The next 2 hours pass in what seems like a couple of seconds.

Rob tells me about the break-up of his marriage, his son and the difficulties of being separated from him by hundreds of miles. I tell him about my divorce and how my daughters and sister kept me sane over the darkest period of my life.

I feel like I've known him for years.

All too soon we have to leave. As I fall back into the dinky toy (with slightly more panache it has to be said), I'm wondering (a) what the likelihood is of the relationship going anywhere and (b) if it does, what my chances are of persuading him to swap the car for something a little less like a big yellow roller skate – a bubble car will do, just as long as I can get in and out of it).

As we arrive back at the College, he discreetly parks right at the end of the top car park showing that he's not completely insensitive (ok it's further to walk but I'm less likely to be the subject of countless dits for the rest of the term!) Before we begin the extracting procedure, Rob leans over and kisses me again and yep, it's official, the tingling is most definitely still there.

As Rob walks me back to The Corridor entrance, he tells me that he's spending the rest of this week preparing the cadets in St Vincent Squadron for The Visit and then next week he's up on Dartmoor for ABLE (remember bleak inhospitable Leadership Exercise ...) I enthusiastically tell him that I'll see him up there and briefly recount the reason why. For some reason he seems to find the idea highly amusing. I resist the idea of walking off in a huff (The Corridor is *so* not the place to flounce) but make it clear that I find his hilarity slightly offensive. He sobers up acceptably quickly but there is a suspicion of a grin lurking under the serious demeanour.

"Well, it wasn't what I had in mind for a possible second date," He says ruefully, "But you never know, we might get to meet up over a nice patch of peat bog and grab a cup of coffee while admiring the view. However, on the off chance that we don't actually get the opportunity for such a romantic assignation, can I give you a call when I get back – maybe for dinner?"

He wants to see me again...

Makes me want to do things to him that have nothing to do with hitting. "I'd pick dinner over a peat bog any time," I respond with a smile, "So you can call me anyway."

Then I turn my back and walk slowly up The Corridor using my perfected Marilyn Monroe walk (really effective in this skirt...)

I don't hear the door open and close until I reach the stairs!

1730 Have spent the rest of the afternoon putting the finishing tweaks to my speech. The Language School has been blissfully quiet as the International Cadets have been given the afternoon to begin preparing for International Day (think their enthusiasm is more because they've been excused from Wednesday afternoon sports).

I'm finding it pretty difficult to concentrate. Silly car or no silly car, I'm beginning to realise that Rob is seriously getting under my skin and the prospect scares the pants off me.

I glance down at Nelson snoring away at my feet. "You've been the only man in my life for so long mate," I murmur, bending down to scratch his tummy. "I'm not sure I know how to let another one in."

His unsympathetic response is to break wind – loudly. Maybe I was a bit too rough on his stomach (very glad it's after five so little likelihood of anyone coming into the office).

1735 While it might have been effective in putting an end to my brooding, the smell is so bad it drives even me out of the office and I decide it's time to go home. Think I'll take Nelson for a bit of walk before we get into the car though, could well slip into a coma if he lets rip with another one of those while we're in the ferry queue.

Thursday 15 October

O730 In the office bright and early to make sure everything English Language related is under control ready for The Visit. I've left Nelson at home with my mum today (for obvious reasons). An arrangement he's perfectly happy with (for obvious reasons).

The College is a whirl of activity. Prince Charles is due to arrive by helicopter at 11am. He is scheduled to meet and greet The Commodore first, then he'll have a quick chat with the cadets standing to attention on the parade ground before being introduced to the other movers and shakers (in order of importance I assume - funnily enough I'm not in that part of the programme).

My moment of fame (or shame) will come when he's escorted on to the Quarterdeck to have a look at the Internationals. Then it's on to meet a (select) few of the British cadets before being whisked away for lunch at the Commodore's house.

I have been briefed fully on how I should greet his Royalness. Apparently when first introduced, I am to say "Your Royal Highness," while executing a small curtsy (have been practicing in front of the mirror...) Thereafter, I'm to address him as 'Sir'.

0800 We have a quick staff meeting to check that everything is going according to plan. The teachers will also be on the Quarterdeck 'supervising' the English Language students (not actually very sure whether that's a good thing – must have a private word with Samantha that under no circumstances is she to get her ball out.)

Feeling a bit sick.

1030 No time for Stand Easy today; I'm just about to head down to the Quarterdeck to take up my place. As far as we're aware the helicopter is on route with no delays.

Just got time to touch up my make-up and give a final check in the mirror to ensure I look ok.

I start at the top. Hair looks good (in a French plait again by necessity – I put so much hairspray in yesterday that I looked like the wild woman of Borneo when I got out of bed this morning).

Eye make-up subtle to blend in with my dark red lipstick – really making a statement today, (about what I'm not entirely sure, but the lipstick looks good and goes with my outfit).

Black fitted suit with dark red edging - slightly oriental in style (complete with a side split in the long skirt – sexy but restrained).

And on my feet, simple black courts (with a sensible 2½" heel – really don't want to go arse over tit on the Quarterdeck today…)

I pin my name badge in a prominent position on the front of my suit and I'm ready to go. Then, picking up my speech (and my reading glasses) I head down stairs towards stardom or infamy.

God I could murder a glass of wine…

1040 I wander around the various displays positioned around the edge of the Quarterdeck. I'm pleased to note that all the International cadets really have gone to town, showing an obvious pride in their respective countries. It actually brings a lump to my throat. They all look so much younger than their British counterparts.

A number of British cadets are stationed around the

Quarterdeck looking extremely uncomfortable in their dress uniforms and obviously wishing that they could be in comfortable anonymity outside on the parade ground with the rest of the Cadets who are waiting to greet the Prince as he arrives.

Suddenly we hear the noise of the helicopter. I glance down at my watch – 1056 – and marvel at the perfect timing that always seems to accompany Royal events such as these.

Have I got time for a wee? The noise of the helicopter increases indicating that its landing is imminent and I decide that my bladder will just have to wait. I put my hand in front of my mouth and breathe out quickly checking for bad breath (not that I think I'll get *that* close but if I'm going to be remembered over this, I don't want it to be for halitosis...)

1105 I'm standing next to Commander NTE near the entrance to the Quarterdeck as we wait for the Prince to finish greeting the cadets outside followed by the College PTB. My heart is beginning to slam a bit harder in my chest and I'm clutching my speech in a death grip.
Really really beginning to feel sick and really really *really* need the toilet!

1120 We can hear the party coming up the steps from the parade ground lead by the Commodore. I practice my curtsy while reciting 'Your Royal Highness' under my breath. Commander NTE is looking infuriatingly cool and at ease – obviously he's done this before.

The Commodore appears at the entrance to the Quarterdeck with Prince Charles next to him. I notice that the latter is in full naval uniform and they both pause and come to attention (all naval officers are required to salute on entry to the Quarterdeck of a ship – never really asked why).

Then the Commodore guides the Prince towards our little party.

To my immense relief, Commander NTE steps forward to greet him and I resist the urge to hide behind his back. Instead I plaster a big smile on my face and wait for my turn (still reciting 'Your Royal Highness' in my head – beginning to think I'll be saying it in my sleep tonight).

All too quickly the Commander NTE turns towards me and I step forward and start to curtsy. I'm just about to say the words, when Prince Charles speaks.

I freeze in mid curtsy. What am I supposed to do now? I haven't got my 'Your Royal Highness' in. I straighten up and make to bob down once more. Again we both speak at the same time. Pretty soon I'm bobbing up and down like a duck in a mud puddle while my voice keeps saying "Your Roya...," like some kind of mechanical toy gone wrong.

To make things worse, Prince Charles is looking directly at my chest. I know it's because he didn't catch my name (why oh why did I put my name badge there?)

My face now resembles a tomato, I know that only a few seconds have elapsed but it feels like hours. Please can somebody just put me out of my misery?

The Commodore comes to my rescue by repeating my name and giving the Prince a short rundown of my duties in the College. As I listen to the Commodore speak I resist the urge to kiss him and gather my scattered wits together.

Result? I'm actually able to respond to the Prince's interested questions without appearing to be suffering from a rare form of Tourette's syndrome.

After giving the Prince a rundown on the different nationalities currently studying at BRNC, I lead him to the first display stand (with the Kuwait Navy – devious I know but you always start with the best you've got).

After chatting for a few moments with a couple of the International cadets, Prince Charles says "Your English is very good." And my heart swells with pride – until I hear the response...

"So is yours Sir."

I laugh a little too loudly while fighting the urge to clout the speaker over the head as I gratefully relinquish the Prince to look around the rest of the displays before speaking with individual British cadets.

I feel like I've run a marathon and I haven't even done my speech yet. I glance over and see The Prince standing next to our resident Royal who is bowing enthusiastically with a huge smile on his face.

My heart sinks. Strategic withdrawal seems like the best option and I flee to the toilet.

My bladder relieved, I sit for a moment in the quiet of the toilet stall wondering if I could just stay here for the rest of the day! I pick up my speech and glasses from the toilet floor where I'd plonked them (I know, yuk but I really was desperate) and, taking advantage of the silence, I read through words again and begin to feel my confidence slowly seep back. I really believe that what I do is important and you know what? I'm good at it, and in just a few moments I'm going to prove it.

1130 This is it. My moment. I actually feel strangely calm as I listen to the Commodore speak briefly about the importance of Officer Training at the College. Distantly I note that Prince Charles is paying close attention to the Commodore's words and then I hear my name.

Taking a deep breath, I step forward.

"Your Royal Highness." (At least I've got to say it once) "Sirs, Ma'ams, Ladies and Gentlemen..."

I go on to speak about the vital role that Defence Diplomacy plays in cultivating allies in these uncertain times and the unique function that International Training plays within such complicated global relations (see, I can do serious and intellectual). I then emphasize the importance of maintaining Britain's influence on the world stage and the necessity of being able to actually see the big picture (especially aimed at the British cadets who get frustrated with their Arabic counterparts).

I wrap up by reiterating just how difficult it is for young international cadets to leave their countries (often for the first time) and undertake what is widely considered some of the most exacting military training in the world – in a language that is not their own.

As I finish, I'm rewarded with a smattering of applause (which includes Prince Charles – yey) and I step back carefully (can't see where I'm treading and really don't think a backward somersault would add anything to the occasion!)

The Prince exits the Quarterdeck, and to my delight he stops and congratulates me on my speech, going on to say how lucky BRNC is to have someone working at the College who is so passionate about their job. (I resist the urge to look behind me to see who he's talking about.)

And just like that I'm a triumph. It's obviously only a matter of time before I'm invited to chat to Oprah.

Maybe I should get an agent...

But first things first – I need a glass of wine...

Before heading to the Wardroom I go over to have a chat with the International cadets and give them a well deserved pat on the back (BZ in Navy speak). To a man they have risen to the challenge (and without any staying on board threats either). I feel a surge of pride and wonder whether I should give them the afternoon off as a reward. Then I look over at HRH's cheerful but baffled expression and stifle the impulse...

I decide to let them go for lunch early instead!

1200 Ok I'm ready to hold court (or at least have a drink bought for me). I fully intend to make the most of my fame and fortune (particularly as I know that everyone will have forgotten about it by tomorrow).

To my surprise (and delight) it turns out that Rob was on the Quarterdeck and witness to my oratory triumph! I bask unashamedly in the warm admiration evident in his eyes while flirting outrageously with my horde of fans (ok, so maybe not quite a horde, but there are at least half a dozen).

Think I'll definitely treat myself to some chips for lunch...

1420 Am back in the office and still on cloud nine. I feel as though I could take on the whole world - though, that could just be the second glass of wine. Prince Charles is due to leave in 10 minutes and the whole College is assembling on the parade ground to see him off (obviously giving the helicopter a wide berth – a few headless cadets on a Royal visit would no doubt be considered very bad form). I grab my coat and head outside. The teachers are already in situ with our International cadets lined up behind them. We're pretty much on the periphery this time. I sigh – it looks as though I've had my 5 minutes of fame.

1430 Prince Charles comes out at 1430 on the dot. He makes a quick speech at the top of the steps (mostly drowned out by the helicopter noise it has to be said but I'm sure it was very deep and meaningful). Then he climbs on board and is whisked away.

It's all over...

And with no major casualties. A couple of sprained ankles (hardly worth mentioning) and one cadet fainted on the parade ground - obviously overwhelmed by the whole occasion (or could have been that he was standing to attention for at least an hour before the Prince actually arrived – the RN are nothing if not prepared).

But at least nobody lost their head...

1815 I'm finally home and even the chaotic state of the kitchen (Frankie's obviously been baking) is not enough to ruin my mood - although it is dented a bit when I notice chocolate frosting on the ceiling.

I grab a glass of wine and head down to mum's to tell her of my triumph.

All in all a brilliant day!

Friday 16 October

O830 Feeling a bit flat this morning in the aftermath of yesterday. Everything's gone back to normal. We've already had 2 cadets decide that an early weekend is in order (probably come to the conclusion that a 3 night stay in the Ritz will help them recover from the hectic activity of the last couple of days).

I've brought Nelson in today but after a halcyon day with my mum yesterday he wasn't keen, the clue being the fact that he parked himself outside my mum's door and flatly refused to shift. It took 3 custard creams and a ginger nut to get him in the car (did I say he was stubborn?) He's now sitting on his chair looking at me reproachfully. I'll take him out for a long walk at lunch time – that'll teach him to sulk.

Anyway, onwards and upwards. I've got a meeting with Commander NTE after Stand Easy to discuss our impending visit to Saudi. I think the intention is for us to fly out (First Class – just wanted to say it again) 2 weeks on Sunday – earlier than expected, so I've got a lot to do before then...

1055 On my way to Commander NTE's office. Unfortunately I missed Stand Easy and thus any last minute desperate glory basking with my army of fans before I'm brushed under the carpet and forgotten. However I did bump into Rob on his way out. Seems he's planning to take his son Jack camping this weekend.

In the dinky toy!

I'm impressed. Anyone who can squash 2 days worth of camping equipment in a boot the size of my underwear drawer has definitely got hidden talents (mind you he's probably intending to wear the same clothes all weekend...)

Still, as long as he washes before Monday.

1205 Back in my office after discussing said impending visit to Saudi. Not quite sure how I feel about it (beyond the obvious). We'll be staying in Riyadh for 3 days and during that time I will be present at the Navy to Navy Staff talks (bit like wallpaper is present on a wall) where I will sit quietly until I'm wheeled out to do my English Language Presentation for the King Fahd Naval Academy.

I'm very likely to be the only woman there (no pressure...)

I'm feeling a bit out of my depth if I'm honest. I know there's nothing wrong with having butterflies – it's getting them to fly in formation that's the problem.

1715 The week's finally over and I'm sitting quietly in the office – just me and Nelson. I go over to his chair and get him to shift over so we squash in it together. He's quite willing to plonk himself half on to my lap and he grumbles softly as he gets himself comfortable before sighing loudly and resting his head on my shoulder.

His weight forces me back into the seat (not to mention his doggy smell) but I really don't mind and I take comfort in his warmth and the feeling of connectedness between us. Nelson doesn't need me to be anything other than I am. He doesn't care if I'm a few pounds overweight; whether I'm a fitness buff; if my make-up's on correctly or if I'm doing my job properly. He just loves me as I am. And that's what I want. I want a man to love *me* warts and all.

I wonder if Rob could be that man. Has he got what it takes to see through the public front I put on to the real person underneath?

Can I allow him to see me naked (both metaphorically and physically...?)

Will he ever want me to go camping in the Lotus?

Only one way to find out....

Week 7

Monday 19 October

O745 All the excitement of last week is now well and truly forgotten. We're now in to Week 7 – half way through the term and the language level of a few of our International Cadets is beginning to cause serious concern (and the buck stops here – no panic).

Sadly I can't produce miracles (walking on water definitely not one of my many talents...) I really need to give Commander NTE a heads up as to who is unlikely to make the grade by the end of term, so I've called a staff meeting to discuss our strategy.

Unfortunately HRH is not improving at the pace we'd hoped (he *is* improving – slowly - and if he were to stay with us for the rest of his life, he might well be good enough to complete the RNYOC...) His Embassy (not sure if they've actually mentioned anything to his father) are not going to be happy to hear that their prodigy has not suddenly become fluent.

Still, trying to look on the bright side, he is now able to actually iron and button up his shirt so you could say (if you were really desperate) that we're going in the right direction...

And not just HRH, there are a few others causing concern.

Hence the staff meeting. Think I'll pop over to the Naafi and pick up a few donuts to help morale.

0815 Tea and donuts in hand, we've isolated the cadets who are currently linguistically challenged and devise a cunning plan to ensure that their level of English is good enough when they commence Officer Training (the main gist of which is to inform the PTB that the cadets need to spend another term with us first...)

Not ideal I know. The problem is (and I know I'm repeating myself here) that in theory, all the cadets accepted on to the Pre-RNYOC should have a certain level of English so that they can cope with the more advanced military language.

In theory...

I finish off the meeting by informing Heather and Andy who are accompanying me on ABLE for the day on Wednesday (both drew the short straws) that they should head up to Naval Stores by 1700 today to pick up their gear (we have been informed by the Leadership Department that we have to be fully kitted out before venturing up onto Dartmoor (did I mention that they're not too keen on the idea?)

However, I'm determined not to be put off by their negativity and intend to head up to Stores straight after Stand Easy (really hoping they've got a pair of combats short enough to fit me).

1035 As I head down The Corridor, I can hear the commotion on the Quarterdeck indicating that the cadets are getting ready for their stint on ABLE. Quite exciting really – can't wait to get stuck in (metaphorically speaking you understand).

The Wardroom is bustling, filled for the most part with officers dressed in combat gear. I can see Rob chatting to Commander NTE. It looks important so I don't disturb him. This is the first time I've seen him out of naval uniform. The combats suit him; just needs some blackout paint on his face and he'd look like Bruce Willis.

Did I mention I have a vivid imagination?

Just before he leaves Rob pops over to say hi and asks me if I'm going to Trafalgar Night on Thursday.

Trafalgar Night is a (very) boisterous Mess Dinner held once a year to celebrate the British Royal Navy's memorable victory at the Battle of Trafalgar on the 21 October 1805. Lead by Admiral Viscount Lord Nelson aboard HMS Victory, the defeat of the French and Spanish fleets was possibly the RN's finest hour (Lord Nelson's too apart from the fact that he died at the end of it!) Of course we've never let the French forget it and Nelson is still spoken of reverently in naval circles today (as well as having dogs named after him...)

I can't actually believe I'd forgotten all about it – must have been all the excitement over the last week.

Of course I *am* going, would never willingly miss it. It really is great fun. Over dinner, the battle is re-enacted (obviously not literally) with the enthusiastic participation of the French Exchange Officer (normally takes several glasses of wine and port to get the enthusiasm going mind you) taking the part of Admiral Villeneuve of France.

I tell Rob that if we don't meet Wuthering Heights style on a bleak windswept part of Dartmoor, I'll see him on the Quarterdeck on Thursday night.

Before he goes, he asks me if I'm taking Nelson with me on Wednesday. Apparently lots of the officers take their (well behaved) dogs with them.

I tell him that I hadn't thought about it, but as I walk back down The Corridor, I begin to warm to the idea and picture us both striding out over the moor, man (or rather woman) and beast in total harmony...

Maybe I will take him. But first more important things – I pop in to the Planning Department to plan for Thursday with Sarah.

1200 Have just got back from Stores. They actually had combats in 'very short' – yey. Felt like Ellen Ripley in Alien when I was trying them on (minus the Uzi machine gun and scary dentally challenged 20 foot monster obviously).

The major problem is that my Bergen is probably bigger than I am and it was a challenge just to pick it up. I asked if the sleeping bag was really necessary but was told to ask that again at 3am in the event that I get lost up on Dartmoor (considered myself duly reprimanded – now wondering whether I should actually tether myself to the officer I'll be shadowing…)

My office is crammed full of said survival gear and Nelson for one is not very impressed – especially since most of it is on his chair. He's currently lying at my feet and sighing very loudly each time I accidently kick him.

Actually beginning to wonder whether this really *was* one of my better ideas…

Still, can't back out now.

Think I need a fortifying lunch to get me in proper survival mode (carbohydrates obviously the order of the day).

1400 The College is now like a ghost town. Nearly everyone has decamped up on to Dartmoor.

Which is just as well really as a couple of minutes ago I received the email with the Commando Challenge pictures attached.

I look like something out of the Night of the Living Dead.

I've got 3 days to bury them…

1700 Think I'm going to suggest to John that a drink in the Cherub might be in order. Really beginning to feel a bit bogged down.

And to top it all, Saudi Arabia is less than 2 weeks away. Sometimes alcohol really is the only answer…

Tuesday 20 October

O800 Things are no better this morning – I really don't know what to tackle first.

Since a glass of wine is out of the question this early in the day (even for me!) I think another visit to the Naafi is in order. And, if I go the long way round and take Nelson for a walk I can then convince myself that the donut I'm intending to eat is actually zero calories.

It may be necessary to go the *really* long way round (like right round the College perimeter).

I head out of the College dragging a reluctant Nelson (definitely not sure whether taking him tomorrow is a good idea).

Feeling very self-righteous…

0900 2 donuts later, self-righteousness is replaced by queasiness – along with a healthy dose of guilt. Nelson on the other hand appears completely guilt and nausea free if his snoring is anything to go by. Still, I'll be having lots of exercise tomorrow. I glance over at my comatose dog and make the decision there and then that if I've got to do it, he can too.

1650 I have a quick meeting with Heather and Andy to make sure we've got all our ducks in a row.

We're being picked up outside gym at 0700 tomorrow morning by a member of the leadership team who warned us that if we we're not ready on the dot, he'll go without us (not sure if he was joking – did I mention they're not too keen on the idea?)

2200 I'm all ready. My combat gear is laid out on my bedroom chair and now all I need is a good night's sleep...

2300 Still awake

0130 Still awake

0245 Still awake...

Wednesday 21 October

O655 I'm standing outside the gym looking like an extra from Shaun of the Dead. I've had approximately 3 hours sleep and l feel like death warmed up.

It's also bloody freezing – the weather has decided to turn wintery (I murderously contemplate how many cadets have been ritually sacrificed by the leadership department to try and put us off...)

Nelson is not looking too happy with the situation either. His tail is so far between his legs he could stick it in his mouth and he keeps looking at me reproachfully. I harden my heart. Lassie wouldn't have looked so miserable.

0705 The bastard's late. I *know* he's done this deliberately and I'm determined to get my own back – just not sure how yet. The 4 of us huddle in the gym doorway as I fantasize about my thermals back in my underwear drawer!

Things can only get better...

0900 Finally arrive up on Dartmoor.

It's now raining.

We park outside 'the hut' which is the centre of operations and after grabbing our survival gear, (with no help from our taciturn driver I might add) we head inside. I say 'we', unfortunately Nelson (being a dog – a fact I think he forgets sometimes) is relegated to the porch.

Needless to say, he's not happy.

Inside the hut is cozy and warm and I'm tempted to suggest we just stay here and do crosswords.

The leadership liaison officer is waiting for us and is actually quite pleasant – he even offers us a cup of coffee and he does a really good job hiding his smirk at the sight of me in combat gear (it has to be said, I do look like a Rambo gnome).

2 cups of coffee later morale is back up and we're raring to go (ok that might be a slight exaggeration...)

We head outside and I grab Nelson's lead and we're off to meet up with the team we'll be watching.

But first need to put on the bloody Bergen.
5 minutes later I'm ready. Pack on back and dog in hand – lead me to it...

1030 Things are not going well. It's taken us nearly 20 minutes to locate the team we'll be shadowing and for all that time I've been bouncing around in a Land rover with a completely panicked Nelson doing his best to sit on my knee. Only the Bergen propped up next to me is stopping us both from ending up on the floor.

On climbing down, Nelson is a miserable shivering wreck and looking at me as though he can't believe I could've actually put him through this. I've got no sympathy - my backside feels like it's been used as a punch bag.

Ignoring Nelson, I drag my Bergen back on to my back and glance over at Andy and Heather to see how they're doing. To my disgust, they really appear to be enjoying it.

I'm obviously more of a Champagne and Caviar kind of girl (although, I've never actually had Caviar and to be honest don't really fancy it...)

1045 Ok so we've finally located our team and it includes 4 International cadets – excellent. I shrug off my Bergen (that is I allow it to land on the floor) and get out my notebook and pen.

This is what it's all about. Nelson is tied to the Bergen and appears to have gotten over his travel sickness – indicated by the fact that he's busy sniffing what looks suspiciously like sheep poo. I can almost hear him thinking 'Mmm yummy'.

We listen intently to the task in hand and watch for our Internationals' grasp of the English used. Happily none of them have a look of complete bafflement but I have to say that neither are any of them taking any kind of initiative. I can see the officer's frustration. Every task has a nominated leader who is (obviously) assessed for his leadership qualities and the rest are measured for their ability to function within a team.

In no time the task is completed and I've already made enough notes to create a small novel.

Time for the next stance.

I look around (just on the off chance that anyone fancies carrying my Bergen, but strangely enough no takers) and then I heave the wretched thing back on to my shoulders. I decide to leave Nelson tied to its side – easier than hanging on to him, and just pray that the next stance isn't too far.

1115 Nelson is acting in a suspiciously well behaved manner. His nose is to the ground and he's trailing behind me really nicely.

Not good...

I can't easily turn around to see exactly what he's up to and decide that as long as he's still on the end of the lead, what can go wrong?

Of course I'm about to find out…

I feel a tug on the lead and pause. Awkwardly turning round I see that Nelson has his head in hole. Tutting loudly, I tug on the lead and all of a sudden a rabbit shoots out right past Nelson's nose and my feet.

Nelson of course gives chase.

My shriek is cut off as the lead jerks the Bergen, spinning me around like a top. Then I fall flat on my back with the Bergen underneath me. The lead is still tied to its side with a frantic Nelson panting at the end of it.

I look just like a turtle and everybody is staring and trying very hard not to laugh. Nelson is still urgently tugging on the lead as someone finally comes forward to get me off my back.

However, the Bergen's so heavy I can't get up and I'm left stranded like some kind of granny version of the teenage mutant ninja turtles.

2 more cadets come forward to help get me on to my feet.

Oh God, things can't get any worse can they?

They finally manage to flip me over – extracting me from the sodding Bergen proving to be a mission impossible.

So now I 'm lying on my stomach, trying to lever myself into a sitting position with the continued help of the 2 cadets (I make a mental note that it isn't any of the Internationals – maybe I should re-think my hard line strategy…)

But Nelson has other ideas. He drags on the lead and pulls me head first into a ditch, the bottom of which is a bog (ok not a toilet but just as bad) where I'm now stuck like a plug in a drain pipe.

I'll kill him.

The sniggering has now got louder and I know I distinctly heard the click of a camera.

I'm now seconds away from crying.

Rob's bound to hear about this.

I tug viciously back on the lead as I'm helped out of the muck and Nelson actually has the temerity to look back at me and wag his tail.

I really WILL kill him.

The officer in charge comes over and asks if I want a lift back to the hut. I can tell he's trying so hard not to laugh.

I gather what dignity I have left and wave him away saying that the mud is no consequence.

However, practically all my notes are now unreadable.

1430 We finally arrive at Ditsworthy Warren for the concluding stance of the day. I managed to take copious notes during 2 earlier exercises and the mud has now dried to a hard crust that is covering the front of me from head to foot.

Nelson has behaved impeccably.

Which just goes to show that he knows what bloody trouble he's in.

1445 The gist of this task is that the cadets have to build a temporary shelter for a couple of hundred 'refugees' who've been rendered homeless (not quite sure by what).

It takes about half hour for the team to put up a temporary tarpaulin shelter and although we follow the various team members around, it's very difficult to assess the language used – particularly as it appears to involve lots of shouting of words that we wouldn't actually want to include in any English lessons...

Nevertheless we are now seated inside the resulting 'temporary shelter' and tucking in to Snickers and hot coffee (this is definitely a plus side to doing lots of exercise).

I'm beginning to feel a lot more sanguine about the whole ditch incident – even going so far as to laugh about it a little, which Nelson definitely senses because he's worked up the nerve to sit up and beg for a bit of Snicker (in his dreams).

Then all of a sudden the lights go out...

1530 I'm lying on the floor of the 'temporary shelter' which turns out was a bit more 'temporary' than anybody guessed. The doctor is asking me how many fingers he's holding up.

Apparently one of the poles holding the structure up collapsed directly on to my head

I frown up at him and, resisting the urge to tell him exactly what he can do with his 3 fingers (obviously haven't lost the ability to count which I understand is good news).

There is an egg shaped lump on the front of my head, but according to the doctor, no concussion.

He does insist however, that tramping around Dartmoor for the rest of the day is now out of the question and tells me that a Land Rover is on its way to take us back to the hut.

I resist the urge to cry. This isn't how I'd envisaged the day going at all – not that I'm presently capable of envisioning anything much at all really.

I feel a bit light headed and sick - determined to keep the Snicker down though...

2015 I'm sitting in mum's flat making the most of her fussing. The lump's gone down slightly (hopefully by the time tomorrow night comes it will no longer be the size of a small grapefruit). What's more, my head is no longer playing 'Da Doo Ron Ron' in throbbing time to my pulse – another plus…

I have a tray containing a light snack (all my stomach can take according to the doc, which is a bit unfortunate because I'm starving).

Even more unfortunate – I'm not allowed any wine…

I wonder if I qualify for a day in bed tomorrow. The idea appeals tremendously at the moment – but then I can hardly turn up at Trafalgar night tomorrow night if I do, so work it is. (I'm such a trooper).

Definitely going to have a lie in though.

Oh God, what if I get a black eye…?

Thursday 22 October

1030 Finally arrived in to work after taking my time getting up this morning.

I've had a leisurely shower and done my hair ready for tonight. The lump on my head is turning a delightful shade of purple which (thank you God) has not travelled down to my eye. It's mostly covered by my fringe and anyway, a little purple showing is not necessarily a bad thing (much better to keep the attention on my injury tonight rather than the episode in the ditch – sympathy over humiliation every time).

I am of course staying on board. Nelson is staying with mum...

1600 I've spent the whole day holed up in my office. Have had a gratifying number of emails checking how I am (and asking if I'm going tonight – feeling quite popular).

And I've had a phone call from Rob...

He seemed very concerned and promised to 'look after me' tonight (sounds interesting). No mention was made about the ditch incident – really hoping that any photographs have gone underground.

Just like the ones from the Commando Challenge (don't ask...)

1615 We're having a quick staff meeting to discuss the information collected from our observations yesterday (language ones that is; although to be fair, I'm not averse to playing the brave plucky heroine injured while courageously doing her duty).

I swan in to the staff room, prepared to play my role to the hilt, only to find the conversation suspiciously stops as I waltz in. Everyone is trying very hard to contain their laughter.

I forgot about Andy's mobile phone. Bastard!

1700 Just finished up in the office and heading up to my cabin for a quick shower and pre-Trafalgar Night glass of wine with Sarah (my turn to bring the wine this time – no problem when you're not dragging a reluctant Irish terrier along a parquet skating rink).

My hair's already done so should be ready in record time.

Any Mess Dinner is always an excuse to dress up. The RN officers wear their 'Mess Undress' (always feel a bit sorry for the female officers) and the rest of us ladies get to put on our glad rags.

I have a range of stock outfits that I wheel out for Mess Dinners – the officer population changes pretty regularly so it's not necessary to keep forking out for new rig (thought I'd slip that Navy term in – haven't used one for a while).

My favourite is a long black taffeta skirt which I team with different tops and tonight I'm putting it with a black sleeveless sequined top with a sheer net back. (It's pretty fitted so bit of a struggle to get on – I can only wear it because I've lost a bit of weight, so taking advantage before the Christmas pounds pile back on.) Never thought of it before but this weight thing is a bit like Groundhog Day really...

1815 Ok, so had a shower and my skirt and make up are on (gone for pink lipstick – don't want to overdo the vamp bit with red). Just got the top to pull over my shoulders (why the hell didn't they put a zip in?)

I slide the top over my head taking care not to mess the doo (or wipe off all my painstaking efforts to look like Sharon Stone...)

I manage to get one arm in followed by half of the other arm. Then I'm stuck...

Did mention that I can't wear a bra with this top?

Shit, I'm now wedged with one arm in and one arm half in and I can't move. My boobs are wobbling like a couple of water bombs underneath the hem of the top and I'm seriously beginning to panic.

Why on earth didn't I try the damn thing on last night...?

OMG what the bloody hell am I going to do. I can't ask Sarah to help me – she'll be traumatized for life.

I can feel my face starting to sweat. Calm down Bev, just calm down. I blow upwards through my mouth, trying to get some air to my now shiny nose.

I take a couple of deep breaths – big mistake. There is an ominous ripping sound where my right arm is stuck.

I feel sick.

Sarah knocks on the door and asks if I'm ready for wine. "Just give me a couple of minutes." I shout gaily as though I haven't got a care in the world.

Inside I'm wailing "Oh God, oh God, oh God, please please *please* let me get out of this and I'll never be vain again – ever, ever, ever..."

Well it's now or never. I haven't got anything else to wear so if I rip my top irreparably, I'm going home. I close my eyes and try and practice a bit of meditation (have you ever tried to meditate when you've one arm stuck above your head and your chest exposed to the world...?)

Experimentally I pull my jammed right arm closer to my body

and slowly, slowly *slowly* I slide it upwards through the arm hole of the top...

About 5 minutes and half a ton of sweat later my arm is actually through. I resist the urge to punch the air (really would finish the top off).

Now all I need to do is pull the hem down over my chest...

I'm in! My face is unfortunately red and sweaty but the top is on – and I can't see any rips anywhere. Thank you God, my new resolution not to be vain will definitely start tomorrow.

No idea how I'm going to get it off later – definitely puts any potential hanky panky right out the window. (I briefly envision Rob struggling to pull the offending garment over my head and shudder with imagined humiliation.)

Mind you, might be a good thing – it doesn't do to look too easy! I remind myself that I'm looking for a proper relationship, not a one night stand (although from where I'm standing abstinence wise, a one night stand is actually looking pretty good).

Sarah knocks on the door again and I let her in.

"Bloody hell, what happened to your face?" She unceremoniously plonks herself down on the bed and hands me a very full glass of rosé. "I had a bit of a struggle getting my top on," I respond with the understatement of the year. "Give me a minute and I'll repair the damage."

It actually takes another 10 – the only recourse was to remove it all and start again. Still, by the end of it we're both very mellow and ready for the night ahead.

I take a last look at myself before leaving the cabin and am pleased to note that all signs of stress are now gone – I have a bit of a rosy glow but I think that's from the wine.

Let's get this party started...

1900 The pre-dinner drinks on Trafalgar Night are always held on the Quarterdeck as the whole evening is considered a 'training evolution' for the cadets (yeah right). Then, just before we go into dinner, we all troop up to the Poopdeck balcony to watch the resident Royal Marine Band 'beat the retreat'.

Basically this involves the band marching up and down the Quarterdeck playing some rousing tunes which helps to get everyone in the mood (if they needed any assistance) followed by the lowering of the British Flag at sunset (known as taking down the Colours) while everyone in uniform stands to attention.

It's all very Queen and Country and 'Sun never setting on the British Empire' kind of thing (actually pretty moving when you see it for the first time – can get a bit wearing when you're watching it for the 20th though). Still, all part of tradition and we all know how important tradition is to the RN.

As Sarah and I walk (carefully) on to the Quarterdeck, we're accosted by a gratifying number of officers offering to get us a drink. I opt for red wine (start as you mean to go on).

I glance around but can't see Rob yet in the milling throng of people. The officers and cadets on ABLE only returned to the College earlier today so they must be knackered – but then, this is the Royal Navy and who ever let exhaustion stand in the way of a good party?

I turn my attention back to the officer who has brought my drink and who is also apparently to host me during the dinner – a fresh faced baby Lieutenant who looks about 19. He is gazing at me with admiration and not a little awe - very heady. I flirt outrageously and enjoy the blushes my witty comments are causing (Ok I know I might not actually be quite Sharon Stone, but as 'mature' women go, there's a lot of mileage in the old girl yet...)

1920 I still haven't spotted Rob as we head upstairs to the Poopdeck balcony – I can only hope he's been placed somewhere near me at dinner.

For the next 10 minutes I give myself over to the rousing music and in no time we're all standing to attention while reflecting inwardly on Britain's past glories (or in my case, have I got enough time to pop to the loo before dinner – once sat down at the table, you're there for the duration until the mess president gives everyone permission to 'ease springs'. And believe me, depending on how many toasts there are, it can feel like forever to your bladder...)

As soon as the flag has been dropped, the Band plays one more rousing chorus of 'What shall we do with the drunken sailor' (very appropriate) as they march off the Quarterdeck.

My attentive escort is once again at my elbow and we make our way (slowly) down The Corridor towards the Senior Gunroom where traditionally the Trafalgar Night dinner is held.

After a quick pop to the heads, I am escorted to my seat which thankfully is not on the top table. Once there we remain standing until Grace is said.

My dinner companions on either side are both pretty young, (and male bless them) but opposite me is Rob... He arrives at the table at the last minute and grins at me. I can't help it; I smile broadly back, my delight very evident on my face. "I was beginning to think you weren't coming."

"Problem with one of the cadets." He responds briefly before going on to declare (to my delight). "You are looking absolutely gorgeous."

Both my dinner companions agree wholeheartedly and I bask unashamedly in their admiration. (This is what makes it so nice to work in such a male dominated environment – Naval Officers might all be irritatingly chauvinistic at times, but boy do they know how to dish out the compliments).

2000 Before Rob can say anything further, the Mess President bangs his gavel onto the table and everyone quietens down for Grace.

My seat is gallantly pulled back for me and then we're off. I have a brief look at the printed Order of 'Service' (mainly to check who the Guest of Honour is – I have no idea, and I have to say I'm none the wiser after reading it, but who cares?)

We start off with smoked salmon and minted melon balls (I think they're meant to resemble the cannon balls on board HMS Victory...)

Luckily the wine's only just started flowing so any juvenile firing of said minted cannon balls is fairly restrained.

2035 As the first course is removed, the opening part of the battle is described aloud by a (comparatively) sober cadet. This is accompanied by some ribald obscenities shouted by the French Exchange Officer (obviously now aided by a few glasses of wine) His English is still pretty fluent however, and his Admiral's Bicorn hat is still sitting reasonably straight on his head.

2100 We're now in to the main course – Roast Beef and Yorkshire pudding with all the trimmings in time honoured British tradition. Our token French Officer, Lt Girardeau, is now settling nicely in to his role assisted by several more glasses of wine (although he now appears to be playing Napoleon rather than Admiral Villeneuve, and his English has definitely deteriorated).

2120 As the main course is removed, the height of the Battle is described with more feeling than accuracy by another (now less sober) cadet...

At this point, Lt Girardeau (obviously feeling that his acting skills haven't yet been fully challenged) leaps on to the table (although 'leap' is probably exaggerating it a bit) and waves his ceremonial sword around in what he probably considers in his inebriated state as a fair imitation of hand to hand combat but actually more accurately resembles a rabid chicken!

The Mess President adds to the mayhem by enthusiastically banging his gavel repeatedly while shouting "A forfeit is hereby given to Admiral Vill... I mean er, Admiral Villa er..... The Frog Admiral for his dishonourable conduct."

2130 Luckily the dessert is brought out before further chaos erupts and Lt Girardeau (having fully exhausted his skills as a budding thespian), is persuaded off the table.

Dessert is Poached Pears served with cream and raspberry sauce, and for a while, relative order is restored as everyone concentrates on their pears in an effort to prevent them shooting across the table and splattering someone's wonderfully white dress shirt with a never to be removed raspberry stain (unfortunately the pears don't appear to have been poached for quite long enough rendering them more lethal on the chest front than a bowl full of spaghetti bolognaise).

2145 Pre Cheese and Biscuits sees the culmination of the Battle (depicted in an impressively dramatic manner befitting the greatest Victory in British Naval History) described by a very drunken cadet, whose first choice of career was obviously following in the footsteps of Sir John Gielgud.

And, at long last, the finale... The lights are dimmed as the stewards bring out trays containing the magnificent Chocolate 'Ships-of-the-Line' complete with live Sparklers sticking out from the hulls representing the cannon fire. As the dazzling cakes are slowly paraded around the table, the spectacle is completed by a drummer from the Royal Marine Band providing the cannon fire noise accompanied by lots of cheering and stamping of feet.

I notice that Lt Girardeau is suspiciously quiet during this ceremony – possibly overawed by this British display of chocolate might (or it could be he's fallen asleep in his pears...)

2200 The Ships are removed back to the kitchen (I'm assuming the kitchen staff get to eat them – don't know why they can't have the poached pears instead.)

Still, we finish the meal with cheese and biscuits followed by coffee and mints so probably wouldn't have had room for chocolate cake, (who am I kidding...?)

Once the table is cleared they bring out the Port decanters ready for the toasts and speeches. Unlike most naval officers, I'm not blessed with a bladder the size of an elephant, so I'm now beginning to feel a tad uncomfortable (really shouldn't have had the water along with the wine). Unfortunately though, there's no respite in sight quite yet so I content myself with crossing my legs and hoping for the best (in the olden days, male officers used to bring bottles...)

The Port is passed around the table and I restrain myself to half a glass (I've had a Port hangover – it's the closest I've ever come to wishing for death.)

No one touches their glass until after the 'Loyal Toast' to the Queen which is performed by the Vice President. (Sipping the Port before the toast is not quite a hanging offence, but it's very close...) Unfortunately I didn't know this at my very first Mess Dinner, and had to ask for another glass after polishing off the first one immediately. (While they didn't actually drag me away in chains, I'm convinced that the stigma lead to my one and only Port hangover – that's my excuse and I'm sticking to it.)

My bladder is now beginning to get insistent... I take a deep breath and cross the other leg. Luckily the toast to the Queen is traditionally taken seated (as if we're on board a ship) for which I'm profoundly grateful…

Ok, that's one down and one to go. Just got to get through the traditional Trafalgar Night Toast to Admiral Nelson, then hopefully we'll be given permission to ease springs and I'll be home and dry (pardon the pun).

Unfortunately the Mess President seems in no hurry to get to the next toast and is chatting to the Guest of Honour as if we have all the time in the world. I can't understand it – doesn't he need to use the bathroom for God's sake? Maybe pee bottles are a required part of their Mess Undress. Before I can stop myself, I glance down at my dinner companion to see if he's doing anything suspicious with his trousers…

I'm now struggling to focus on anything but my need for the toilet and I suddenly realize I'm rocking backwards and forwards like one of those toothless old crones that sit knitting by the Guillotine.

The customary Trafalgar Night toast to Nelson is usually done by the youngest person in the room and I try to distract myself by asking Rob who it is. By the time the Mess President gets up to bang his gavel, I'm fantasizing about cracking him over the head with it (the Mess President that is, not Rob.)

Happily the fresh faced Lieutenant who delivers the toast doesn't have a bottle with him judging by the speed at which he shouts the words (there's a definite urgency in his stance that can't be mistaken – I want to kiss him).

This time we have to stand unfortunately and once on my feet, I'm tempted to make a run for it, etiquette be damned…

"To the immortal memory of Nelson and those who fell with him."

And then it's over. I'm back seated on the edge of my chair, poised like a coiled spring...

"Permission to ease spri..."

I'm half way across the room before he gets to the 'gs'!

2215 I feel like a new woman.

Unsurprisingly, I'm first back to my seat and now I'm able to think clearly again, I feel quite sad that I wasn't able to appreciate what is actually normally quite a moving toast. I sip at what's left of my drink and wonder how long the speech is likely to be. The Port will definitely go round at least once more, but I'm now eager to get on to the next part of the evening.

While the dinner has been great fun, I haven't yet had much opportunity to chat with Rob.

Still, the night is young...

2225 The Guest of Honour is an Admiral who is apparently a distant relative of Nelson (not *that* distant though judging by his age).

He starts off talking about Nelson's leadership qualities – quite interesting really.

2245 Still talking about leadership qualities

2255 Talking about somebody else's leadership qualities...

2305 Talking about the *importance* of leadership qualities.

I'm gradually losing the will to live. At this rate we'll be here til morning...

I glance around me and notice several cadets (most notably those who have just returned from ABLE) swaying in their seats in an effort to stay awake. I wonder how long it will be before one of them falls off his chair.

2315 Is this the longest speech on record? I'm beginning to need the toilet again (I'm also beginning to seriously worry that I've got a bladder problem...)

Suddenly everyone starts banging on the table and I realize it's actually finished.

The table banging is a tradition in the RN that stems from not being able to clap with 2 hands when on board a ship rolling on the high seas (for obvious reasons).

On this occasion, it also serves to wake everybody up.

Finally, without wasting any more time, the Mess President gives everyone permission to retire to the bar...

My host gallantly pulls back my chair (luckily I was actually getting up from it at the time). I smile at him sweetly and thank him for a lovely evening. Then I leave Rob talking to a couple of cadets and make my way down the table towards Sarah who's waiting for me at the end.

"Bloody hell, I thought he was never going to finish." I roll my eyes in agreement with her blunt assessment as we head down the steps to The Corridor.

Suddenly a voice murmurs in my ear from close behind me, "What are you having to drink gorgeous?" To my delight Rob appears at my elbow and with a grin, Sarah tactfully disappears...

0120 I am now very pleasantly tipsy. It's been a wonderful evening. Rob has spent the last couple of hours glued to my side despite numerous attempts to drag him into the boisterous Mess games taking place at the other end of the bar.

I can tell he likes me – a lot, and I have to say that the feeling is mutual. I actually feel like I'm floating on cloud nine. Then he asks if I'd like to go back to his cabin for a night cap...

And I want to, I really do, but I just know what it will lead to and even as intoxicated as I am, I can't forget my earlier mental picture of the two of us wrestling with my top – I've read too many romance novels. (I'm sure my vision is not what they meant when they coined the term 'bodice ripper'.)

I can't help it; it has to be exactly right…

So I tell him that I need to be in the office bright and early tomorrow to begin working on my presentation for Saudi and he agrees with a rueful smile to walk me to my cabin instead.

On the way he asks again if I like sailing and I nod my head enthusiastically (probably a bit more squiffy than I thought…)

He does seem a little surprised at my fervent response (which to be fair was a bit over the top) but undeterred goes on to ask if I fancy the idea of sailing to the picturesque port of Salcombe with him when I get back from the Middle East.

"We'll have to stay overnight on the yacht," He clarifies carefully without looking at me, "But I'd really love to take you".

I'm positive my heart actually swells with happiness and turning towards him, I pull his head down to kiss him gently on the lips. Looking directly into his eyes, I whisper, "I'd love to," with a smile.

I just know it will be perfect…

Week 8

Thursday 29 October

O 815 So far the week has gone by in a complete blur. I feel as though the only time I've come out of my office is to eat, sleep and visit the toilet.

Needless to say, as always, Nelson is not happy.

He keeps looking at me reproachfully with his hang dog, 'my life is pants' expression to remind me that he hasn't had a decent walk in 3 days (actually I'm not sure it's the walk bit, more like I haven't been over to the Naafi to keep him supplied with ginger nuts and donuts).

I am resolutely ignoring him however, his girth is expanding along with mine and now the Commando Challenge is a distant dream (or nightmare) we could both do without the added carbs.

And anyway, I haven't got time to eat.

Still, my determination (I'd like to say enthusiasm but that vanished around Tuesday teatime) has got me through and I now have the first draft of my Saudi English language presentation. It should only take me another twenty hours or so to perfect it.

I've got one more day…

Panicking a bit actually – maybe a donut would help me (quick rush of sugar – give me the extra brain power…)

Mind you, it's Shareholders today, so if I hang on, I can in all good conscience take a biscuit break. I look down at Nelson who sighs dramatically – sometimes I swear he can hear my thinking...

10.30 I resolutely take off my glasses and, after promising Nelson I'll bring him back a biscuit, I head out of my office before I change my mind.

As I throw open the door, I startle a few of the students who are just starting their stand easy. They look at me for a second as if wondering who I am (I haven't been holed up in my office for that long... Possibly they thought I was dead – or hoping anyway.)

They drone out their 'Good morning Ma'am' less than enthusiastically as they troop by. I sigh – they don't seem any more regimented than the day they first walked in.

Can't think about that – got too much on my plate at the moment.

I haven't even seen Rob all week. Apparently he's in Portsmouth until tomorrow. I know I've said it before but it's true - every time things seem to be hotting up, he promptly disappears.

Maybe it's a sign...

Truth is though, I'm also a bit worried about the whole sailing thing. My enthusiasm was definitely down to 2 things:

1. Spend time with Rob alone

2. Possible end of enforced celibacy...

But I've never even been on anything smaller than a frigate (and then it was in the middle of the River Dart),
and the furthest I've been in the English Channel was 20 years ago when I went for a quick paddle on Paignton beach.

I'd definitely rather spend time alone with him in a 5 star hotel along with a queen sized bed and a hot tub.

Don't think that was quite the impression I gave though, if my somewhat hazy recollection of the end of Trafalgar night is correct.

And what if the weather's bad? It will be November for God's sake... I'm now envisioning 10 force gales with me clinging on to the yard arm (what is a yard arm anyway?) dressed in sou'wester and gumboots while Rob stands at the helm fighting to keep us afloat...

I shake off my feelings of impending doom – it's not the bloody Titanic for pity's sake; I'll be singing a rousing chorus of 'My Heart Will Go On' next if I'm not careful.

And anyway, I'm now at the bottom of the stairs and need to concentrate on negotiating The Corridor – breaking my leg just before going to Saudi is not likely to enhance my meteoric rise to the highest echelons of the Company (especially if I do it due to my unsuitable footwear...)

10.35 I grab my coffee and surreptitiously stuff a couple of biscuits in my trouser pocket for Nelson later (that's how stressed I am – can you believe it? I'm actually wearing trousers...) Then I look around to see who's here to chat to. Although I've been closeted in my office for so long, everyone's probably forgotten who I am)

I'm just beginning to get to that uncomfortable period –the one a few minutes after you've arrived somewhere and realise that you don't know anyone and you're wondering whether you should just blend into the wall -when I gratefully spot Sam heading towards me, coffee in hand. We chat happily for a few minutes and I wonder briefly whether I might have gone for the wrong officer but then a familiar voice murmurs in my ear, "Hi gorgeous, how's it going?" And my heart does a little flip...

I'm just about to ask him why he's back so early but Sarah joins us and the opportunity is lost. Hopefully we'll get to chat before the coffee morning's over.

10.45 He's still talking to Sam

10.50 He's still talking to Sam

10.55 He's STILL talking to Sam

Now call me self centred, but I'm now figuring that he can't want to speak to me *that* badly.

Maybe he doesn't want to talk to me at all – could well be a sign…

11.00 I can't put it off any longer (and believe it or not, I really *do* want to knock their proverbial tea towels off in Riyadh) so I swallow my frustration and turn to walk off the Quarterdeck with Sarah.

"Bev." Rob calls my name after I've gone a few steps and, after pausing for a second, I tell Sarah I'll catch up with her later and turn back slowly with feigned nonchalance. If this guy thinks he can pick me up and put me down whenever he wants, then he's sadly mistaken. (You know, back to the whole I'm Every Woman thing again…)

I stay where I am and simply raise my eyebrows (hopefully I'm not too far away to ruin the effect) and wait for him to come to me.

He comes over gratifyingly (one could even say life threateningly) quickly - remember, leather shoes… and I feel my annoyance dissipate a little.

Only a little…

"Sorry about that." He really does sound contrite.

"I thought you weren't back to work until tomorrow," I respond, my tone still pretty brusque.

"I wanted to see you before you went off on your Arabian

adventure so I came back a day early."

And just like that, my earlier irritation melted away. "Are you allowed to do that?" I quip in a much softer tone.

"I'm back in Portsmouth all next week so it's no big deal and I wanted to arrange our sailing trip before you got your head turned by some mega rich sheik.

"I was thinking that maybe we could go next weekend if you're free?"

I pause briefly, fear of possible drowning still warring with possible end of enforced celibacy...

"Of course, that's subject to the weather," He goes on hurriedly (is my face that easy to read...?) "We won't go if it's bad, but the long range forecast is actually looking pretty good at the moment. We'll stay overnight in Salcombe and I know a lovely little fish restaurant that I really want to take you to in the evening..."

Who needs a queen sized bed and a hot tub anyway?

Definitely a sign!

Friday 30 October

1 715 Ok that's it. I shut down my computer, pick up my 'Saudi' folder and head home to pack...

I'm meeting Commander NTE (call me Steve) on Sunday afternoon at Heathrow Airport (did I mention 'Steve' and I are flying First Class..?)

Our 'First Class' flight leaves at 1700 which gets us into Riyadh at approximately 0240 in the morning local time (nothing like arriving dewy eyed).

Still, we'll have the whole of Monday to get over the jet lag and soak in the sights (well at least 'Steve' will, not sure if I'll be allowed out of my hotel room).

I don't think the airport is too far away from the city and we're being met by someone from the British Embassy (I hope).

Now all I need to do is to find something to wear which, to be fair, is not really a major problem as I'll be the only person who sees what I've actually got on. Apparently our driver is going to bring me a black 'abaya' and head scarf to put on when we land.

I've got blond hair – never thought of it before. Should I have had it dyed? Is my hair colour more or less likely to get me carried off into the desert?

And why am I being so stupid – I'm a professional! And surely I can't possibly be the first female to address the Saudi Navy...?

Saturday 31 October

1920 Finished my packing – everything in there is black with sleeves covering both my elbows and my ankles. You never know, I might have to go into hospital and I need to cover all my bases.

Not sure about my basics though – all my black underwear would definitely not go down well in a Saudi hospital...

Think I'll stick with my white sensible Marks and Spencer twin sets.

Frankie is cooking me dinner tonight – it feels a bit like the last meal of a condemned man; Rosie, James and my mum are coming...

Still if anything happens to me, at least I won't have to clear up the aftermath.

2250 Have had a lovely evening. Frankie cooked us all a gorgeous meal and as she sensibly chose to do a casserole, there wasn't too much washing up (however, the casserole dish is likely to be in soak until I get back...) I drank a little too much wine and not just because it's doubtful I'll be getting any over the next few days.

And I've had a text from Rob wishing me luck. He's back from Portsmouth next Friday and I've taken the plunge and asked him if he'd like to call in for supper on his way through on Friday evening.

I was half hoping he'd say no but he seemed very keen and said he'd aim to be here for 1930 (they really do take this 24 hour clock thing seriously in the military...)

So now I've given myself 2 added problems to agonise over:

1. What should I cook?

2. Should I make Frankie go out or would it be better to get the meeting over with earlier rather than later?

Oh and one last thing; need to make sure the flat's not like a scene out of world war 3 when I get back Thursday evening...

2355 OMG, just remembered, I need to put my clock back one hour for the end of British Summer time – bloody hell, close call... (Mind you, at least it's going the right way).

Sunday 1 November

1300 Finally on the Paddington to Heathrow shuttle train. I breathe a sigh of relief. I'm meeting Commander NTE – sorry, Steve – at 1400 next to the British Airways check in desk (that's the First Class one...) so there's no rush.

I can finally relax a little.

1430 Am now sitting in BA's Premier lounge. Our cases have been checked in and I'm now looking at a (free) glass of champagne. I actually feel a bit like one of the Waltons.

I take a surreptitious glance at Steve who has his head buried in the newspaper (anybody would think he feels a bit awkward). He certainly doesn't seem fazed by the actual first class experience at all - think it's more that he's having it with me! I notice that he's already downed his glass of bubbly, so I pick up my glass, determined to keep up...

1615 3 glasses of champagne and numerous (small) canapés later, we're ready to board. 'Steve' has definitely loosened up a little and although my voice has risen an octave, he doesn't appear to have noticed, so all in all things are looking up.

First Class (I know I keep repeating myself but give me a break – this may never happen again) is situated at the front of the aircraft and unbelievably it's full. We're shown to our seats which apparently lie down flat should we decide to sleep. (I resist the urge to test mine.) I do, however, succumb to bouncing up and down a little and stretching my legs out as far as they'll go (still another couple of feet – it's amazing). There are more little canapés situated in a small tray next to our seats and we are handed another glass of champagne before we've even left the tarmac.

I really need to eat something substantial…

I look around me; everyone just seems to be taking all this in their stride. They probably do it every week.

It seems that I'm the only one excited about the little goody bags we're given. Mine's got a toothbrush, little tube of toothpaste, a grooming set and a silky eye mask just like the one Joan Collins wore in Dynasty (showing my age again).

Then we begin to move in preparation for takeoff and, stuffing my goodies back into the bag, I notice that the cabin staff are coming round to take back the champagne glasses. I've only half finished mine, so I down the rest in one and stuff the remaining canapés into my mouth.

Result? I'm unable to do anything more than stare dumbly up at the stewardess as she takes my glass and asks me if I'd like any red or white wine once we're in the air.

I glance quickly at Steve who is raising his eyebrows encouragingly at me.

If I open my mouth to say anything half sodden lumps of smoked salmon blinis are likely to be decorating the front of my shirt and hers. I frantically try to chew without moving my mouth (have you ever tried to do that?)

I daren't swallow, so resign myself to looking up at her with an attempt at a smile without showing my teeth while nodding vigorously.

"Would that be red or white?" She looks back at me patiently.

I try an experimental swallow and eventually I'm able to croak out "Red please," like a ventriloquist without a dummy.

"Would you like some water with your wine madam?" Her face is deadpan and politely enquiring.

My face is now matching the beautiful silk scarf she wears around her neck as I nod my head without looking at Steve who is now (thank God) examining the in flight safety procedures. I want to ask him if there's anything in there on choking to death while taxiing down the runway...

Luckily the stewardess is called back to her seat for takeoff and I'm able to furtively deposit the rest of my champagne mush into a tissue and take a deep breath. Leaning back into my seat, I close my eyes while thinking reverently, "Thank you God. I promise I will never try to speak with my mouth full again (and I will further promise that I will make a concerted effort not to overfill my mouth through greed, gluttony or fear of missing out).

1800 We're now safely in the air. My wine (and water) is on the tray in front of me and I'm examining the menu.

Yes, there is a menu. And not only that, but real knives and forks. (I was definitely born for this.)

I decide to go for the fillet steak diane followed by sticky toffee pudding (on the outside possibility that I get locked up for going through the airport without my abaya, I might need some fat on me...)

Steve is now on his third glass of wine and I'm seriously impressed. In fact I'm firmly convinced that one of the requirements for promotion in the RN is to be able to drink copious amounts of alcohol without passing out. Maybe he's stocking up for the 3 day drought to come?

Anyway, it's made him a lot chattier and we're now getting along famously. In actual fact, I never realized before, but he's really quite witty (mind you, that could be because I'm now on my second glass of wine).

1900 (or is it now 2200 – when does the time actually change?) Steve's now on his second glass of Port and my admiration is turning to awe. Or it would do if I could keep my eyes open (it definitely feels more like 2200).

Don't think I'll bother with coffee.

Time to test the bed...

And the eye mask of course.

Week 9

Monday 2 November

O030   I wake up and for a second I wonder if I'm dead because I can't see anything. Then I remember to take off the eye mask and I notice is that the cabin lights have been dimmed. I glance over at Steve who is snoring softly beside me – it feels oddly intimate actually and I hastily bring my chair into a sitting position while scrubbing at the now dried up drool that is decorating my cheek.

I don't think I've been snoring! (I've never actually heard myself but Frankie assures me I snore like a walrus although I'm sure she's exaggerating).

I feel pretty grubby and despite the nice silky eye mask, my eyeballs feel as though they've got boulders in them.

Lesson learned – doesn't matter whether you're in first or cattle class, whether you've been given your own toothbrush or not, you still feel scabby when you fly.

I glance down at my watch. By my reckoning we've still got a couple of hours to go – maybe it's time to try out my own personal TV...

0215 We're starting our descent into Riyadh. Everyone is now appropriately bright eyed and bushy tailed and ready to land. I've used my little goody bag to freshen up (and remove all my make-up; no red lipstick for the next 3 days...) As I look around, it seems that some people have done much more to prepare for landing. There are a couple of ladies sat opposite us who started the flight wearing Gucci's finest and now appear to be ending it so that not even their husbands will be able to recognize them.

I have time to briefly wonder how it all works when couples go shopping – how does hubby spot his wife in the supermarket when they all look the same...)

I'm now really feeling nervous and very glad for Steve's solid presence beside me.

0250 We're walking through the airport towards the Saudi Border Control and I feel as though absolutely everyone is staring at me. There are hardly any women around and those that are present are completely covered up from head to toe. My hair stands out like a beacon (why oh why didn't I bring a head scarf with me – or better yet, dye it black?)

My heart is thumping erratically and I can feel the sweat beginning to slip between my shoulder blades. I have to resist the urge to hide behind Steve's back.

As we get to the border control, Steve (of course) is allowed straight through but I'm taken into a small room where they examine my paperwork while chatting at each other in Arabic.

I feel sick. I am taken into another room where a woman (I think it's a woman but can't be sure as even her eyes are covered up with a black cloth – I wonder slightly hysterically how she'll be able to tell if I'm carrying anything illegal...)

I can see Steve waiting anxiously at the other side of the barrier – he might as well be on the other side of the world.

Holding my arms out, I take a deep breath and allow the person in front of me to check me over for anything forbidden.

I can see through a small window that they now have my suitcase and I'm seriously beginning to sweat (even though I know there's nothing in it that shouldn't be). (OMG are women allowed to bring Evening Primrose Oil into the country?)

My imagination has now got me locked up in a damp cell with nothing more than a bucket and a mattress – in fact I've already lost half a stone...)

Then, all of a sudden, it's over. With a curt nod, the guard dismisses me and I'm allowed to drag my case through customs.

I fight the urge to throw my arms around Steve's neck while blubbering into his shoulder (definitely not a good look for a professional woman of the world) and content myself with a few sniffles (it *is* 3am).

At that moment our escort to the hotel arrived (where the hell was he 5 minutes ago...?) He shakes hands with me as well as Steve (not always a given in Saudi) and then hands me my abaya.

It's at least a foot too long (all over). Who was the last wearer of this thing – whoever it was would have given Goliath's mother a run for her money.

I spend the next few minutes flapping around trying to get my hands free of the sleeves so I can do it up at the neck while our escort waits impatiently holding out my headscarf. I shove the sleeves up past my elbows and, grabbing the scarf, place it on my head, crossing the ends over at my throat and leaving them to trail down my back.

My sleeves have dropped down again. I shove them back and grab hold of the front of the abaya in an attempt to lift the hem off the floor.

I look like a demented Winnie the Witch.

I'm never going to be able to manage my case. I look helplessly at Steve. Our escort is already striding away.

Any minute now I'm going to simply sit on the floor and start bawling (I don't bloody care if I'm a professional woman of the

184

world…)

Luckily Steve takes charge. He tells me to stay put with the luggage and chases after our departing escort.

I don't know what he said but whatever it was, it did the trick and quick as a flash our reluctant aide is back by my side, all apologies and taking my case from me.

I trail after them both, trying to keep my headscarf on with one hand and holding the front of the abaya out of the way of my feet with the other. Despite my best efforts, I keep tripping over the hem and am now walking like Quasimodo in a black dressing gown. Any minute now I'm going to start clutching my head and moaning 'Oh the bells, the bells…'

I'm getting hysterical – definitely need to go to bed.

0330 I'm finally sitting in the back of the car that will take us to the hotel (I hope). I can't believe that only a few short hours ago I was sipping champagne without a care in the world.

I want to go home!

0930 It really is true, things definitely look better in the bright light of day! I woke up this morning feeling much less like my get up and go had got up and gone.

My hotel room is really rather splendid (old fashioned word I know, but actually it truly is). All grand marble and beautifully woven tapestries. It's on the 9th floor with an amazing view over the city of Riyadh. From my hotel room I can see The Kingdom Tower looming imposingly over the city and the Ministry of Interior Building which pretty much resembles an upside down space ship.

Talk about stepping outside of your comfort zone…

I feel a renewed sense of excitement – I'm actually looking forward to whatever experiences the day brings (that's if I don't break my neck in the bloody abaya first).

I'm supposed to be having breakfast with Steve before getting together with the resident Naval Attaché to discuss tomorrow's strategy (that is, they'll talk and I'll listen).

1100 Sitting in the hotel lobby with coffee and biscuits. Breakfast was amazing. We sat outside on the terrace in beautiful 23 degree sunshine. The high point was the maple syrup pancakes and the low point was nearly setting fire to my sleeves reaching over the warming plate (the smell of smoldering nylon was not pleasant I can tell you).

The Naval Attaché (a very jolly Naval Commander – call me 'Mike') has promised to bring me another one that actually fits. Probably concerned about the possible insurance bill if I have to wear this thing for much longer...

Apparently I don't have to wear my head scarf inside the hotel which is great.

So, here we are with coffee and biscuits – obviously not allowed to dunk.

I sit trying to look interested as they discuss various dits that have both of them laughing uproariously (apparently strategy is coming later over dinner). The problem is that I don't know what or who the hell they are talking about and after my late night (or early morning – depending how you look at it) my eyes are beginning to glaze over.

Finally, I can't stand it any longer – it's either retire to my room or snuggle down with my head in Steve's lap...

I opt for retiring to my room.

Apparently we are going to have a look round the Souks in the old part of Riyadh later on this afternoon. 'Mike' is coming to collect us and has promised faithfully to bring me another abaya in 'extra short'.

1500 It fits – yey!   And just to make sure there's no further surreptitious trailing of sleeves (or of me going up in a puff of smoke), the cuffs actually do up. The length is also perfect – I think maybe the number 12 on the inside label refers to the age of the last wearer rather than the size.

There's no mirror for me to look at myself (probably a good thing) so I simply tie my head scarf over my head and hurry after the men who are already striding towards our car waiting outside (I'm noticing a definite trend developing here...)

1700 I feel like Billy no mates.

We've done the sightseeing tour and are now sitting outside a local coffee shop. Steve and Mike are sitting together on a table about 20 feet away.

And I'm sitting on my own. Apparently, being members of the opposite sex, we're not allowed to sit together. In fact we can't actually make eye contact, let alone talk...

The 'Adhan' calling Muslims to prayer begins to sound over loud speakers in the nearby mosque.

I shiver a little – it all feels so strange – like another world.

Even another planet...

It's been a very long day!

Tuesday 3 November

O830 I'm lying in bed feeling pretty homesick. I feel very apprehensive about my contribution towards the staff talks today.

Mike was actually speculating in our 'strategy' meeting last night that I could well be the first woman to ever have stepped inside the Royal Saudi Naval headquarters.

No pressure…

Still, can't spend too much time analyzing. Mike is coming over to the hotel for breakfast along with the assistant Naval Attaché so I'm going to have to get weaving.

Mind you, won't take me long to decide what to wear…

1000 Breakfast was light hearted and fun which is exactly what I needed to take away the nerves. The hotel staff are really friendly (albeit all male) so beginning to relax again.

1030 Scratch that, I'm not relaxed at all. Currently sitting in the back of the car taking us to the Royal Saudi Naval Headquarters.

I resist the urge to ask Steve to hold my hand.

I need a wee…

1048 We're having coffee and biscuits while waiting for the Saudi Admiral to arrive. Or rather, everyone else is -I'm sitting in a corner trying to look inconspicuous (not really that difficult to be fair).

There are 12 men and me. My head scarf kept falling off so I've resorted to tying it tightly around my neck. If the end gets caught on something there's a good chance I'll be garroted.

And there aren't any ladies toilets - think I might have to consider doing some exercises to increase bladder control.

1105 The Admiral arrives and we're escorted into the meeting room. There are now 20 men and me. There aren't enough chairs around the table so I'm relegated to sitting against the wall giving a whole new meaning to the word 'wallflower.

1300 We're having a break for lunch. They're going to talk about Naval Training after eating and that'll be my cue - I'll be wheeled out to talk about English Language Training for their trainee cadets. I wonder briefly if I'm supposed to remain where I am and eat my lunch off a tray but apparently not; I'm beckoned to accompany everyone and trail after them feeling completely out of my depth.

I catch up to Steve to ask him in a whisper what I'm supposed to do about the toilet. He has a word with his opposite number, who has a word with the Admiral's aide and pretty soon everyone is scratching their heads looking a bit nonplussed.

I can't believe no one thought of this – and I really, *really* need the toilet (I have actually lasted over 3 hours which I think might be a record for me since I hit 40).

At length I am given permission to use the Admiral's private loo. By this time they could have offered me a hole in the ground and I'd have said thank you.

1320 All ablutions taken care of, we all troop into a large beautifully appointed formal dining room.

There are now 60 men and me...

I'm seated opposite a very pleasant gentleman who is not in uniform (no bloody idea who he is) but he's very polite and seems happy to chat to a woman. He tells me that he loves going to London and does so at every opportunity – usually 4 or 5 times a year. I nod respectfully as he continues to tell me about his favourite hotel – the one that he always stays in. Have I heard of it? It's called The Dorchester!

He asks me if I've ever stayed there and when I shake my head he advises that I ask my husband to take me at the earliest opportunity...

Maybe a rich sheik carrying me off into the desert wouldn't be so bad after all.

1400 Beginning to think that the lunch is never going to end. They have brought out course after course – all delicious. Or would be if I had any appetite.

Unfortunately I'm too nervous to eat much.

1415 Lunch is finally over and we're given a bit of a reprieve as everyone goes off to pray, leaving the four of us Brits to wait back in the conference room. I dig out my presentation and put it on to the laptop ready. Seriously beginning to get heart palpitations now.

Wish I could have a drink.

1510 They've spent the last half an hour discussing the merits of training the most 'gifted' Saudi officer cadets at BRNC and now all eyes are looking my way - it's up me to talk about possible English Language Training.

It's finally time to rock and roll...

1600 It's over at last. We're on our way back to the hotel and I can relax for the first time in days.
My presentation actually went very well considering listening to

women is not an activity done that often in Saudi Arabia.

I'm going to have a lie down!

1900 We're being taken out for dinner to (possibly) the only restaurant in Riyadh which allows women to eat in a public place – exciting...

2200 A very interesting evening. Basically we sat in a booth with a curtain over the entrance so that any other 'male' diners would not be tempted by my presence. (I know I can do pretty hot when required but I would very impressed if any member of the male species found me attractive dressed up like a Darth Vader groupie.)

Still, quite flattering really – just wouldn't want to do it more than once.

Wednesday 4 November

O 900 Going home tonight and I have to say that I'm really looking forward to getting back to good old Blighty. This has been an amazing experience, but, to quote Judy Garland, 'There's no place like home'

And Riyadh most definitely ain't Kansas!

A car is coming to pick us up at 1830 as we're being hosted at the British Embassy this evening before flying out at 2310 local time. That means we've got about 9 hours to kill before checking out of the hotel. Mike suggested shopping in the mall at the bottom of Kingdom Tower, and as you are no doubt aware, I'm never averse to a spot of retail therapy.

Might be a bit awkward going with Steve though (mind you, I'm definitely not going on my own...)

1100 Just discovered that they have every shop that we have in the West and more. In fact, apart from 2 glaring facts, I could be anywhere in Europe – it's so bizarre.
The 2 glaring facts? There are absolutely no changing rooms in any of the boutiques and there are absolutely no female shop assistants *anywhere in any shop.* It was majorly weird walking around Debenhams with male shop assistants trying to sell us perfume.

To be fair, there is a second floor which is apparently 'for women only'. It's actually guarded by men with guns.

I'm so ready to go home...

1600 Am now lying on my bed having a rest before heading out to the Embassy and possible gin and tonic time? I did actually manage to buy myself some very nice earrings and helped Steve choose some perfume for his wife (just managed to save him – and possibly his marriage - from buying 'Youth Dew' – I'm assuming his wife is not over 70).

I've also realized that all abayas most certainly do not look the same.

There are all kinds of styles – some costing thousands. It's absolutely amazing how intriguing a pair of beautifully made up eyes look over the top of a black silk 'hejab' (apparently that's the correct word for the head scarf and face covering used by Arabic women.)

Some women also had their hands hennaed along with gorgeous nails.

Maybe there really is something to this whole 'covering up lark'.

Particularly, if you're 5ft7, massively rich and have eyes like Sophia Loren...

It seems that women the world over are not that different – we all do the best with what we have.

1815 We've checked out of the hotel and are now being driven (could actually get used to this) to the British Embassy for drinks and nibbles...

1945 Am on my second gin and tonic and wearing jeans and a t-shirt.

I feel like a new woman.

The Embassy employees are really lovely and great fun to be around. They've also given me another side to the whole living in Saudi thing - such as the benefits of being able to go shopping without actually taking off your pyjamas...

I think Embassy functions are probably the only times they can really let their hair down.

2045 Finally on our way to the airport – yey.

2250 Just about to board. Been frisked 3 times by possible women (no exotic eye make-up here) but think at the end of the day they're probably glad to get rid of me.

All things considered, I don't think 'Professional Women of the World' are very popular in Saudi Arabia!

Thursday 5 November

1500 Am actually feeling pretty good considering I spent the whole of the night travelling – can't really remember much of the flight back as I slept through most of it (didn't even drink much – that's what going without alcohol for nearly 3 days does to you, you become a complete lightweight).

Feeling a bit peeved that I didn't make the most of the return journey though – not sure if the company will cough up again (especially if nothing comes of it...)

Still I did get to use the British Airways First Class lounge when I arrived back in Heathrow. I had a shower and a full English breakfast before catching the train back to obscurity...

And now got the day off so I'm making the most of it before reporting back to the PTB tomorrow.

Means I can also get back to some important stuff...

Namely, what am I going to 'cook' (I use the term loosely) for Rob tomorrow night and of course, more crucially, what am I going to wear?

I'm trying very hard not to think about my upcoming sailing adventure (apart from the possible adventures of the night of course...)

Friday 6 November

1600 It's official, I was a success in Riyadh – I really was.

In fact so much so that the Saudi Royal Navy have already indicated that they want us to put together an English Language 'Summer School' at BRNC for 60 officer cadets from the King Fahd Naval Academy...

60 male teenagers from Saudi Arabia – here, all at the same time.

Can't wait... (It's true; sometimes success does come at a price).

Still, it also means that I can, with good conscience, leave work early to go do some shopping for my culinary masterpiece tonight. (Otherwise known as chilli con carne.)

Ok, so I know it's a bit dated, boring etc – but my chilli does taste bloody good. And more importantly I can get it done in advance (which is all good for obvious reasons!)

1830 Said culinary masterpiece is now sitting on the stove ready. I've just got time for a quick shower before Rob arrives at about 1930 (have had a text saying he's on his way from Portsmouth, which obviously means he's still coming...)

Quite nervous actually. And not just because I've found out that Frankie's not going out until later so introductions are inevitable...

But at least the flat's tidy.

1925 Ok I'm all ready. Nice ambience in the living room; a few scented candles scattered around (helps disguise the smell of dog a bit...) and strategically placed lamps. I've got a lovely view over the bay from my living room balcony which is sure to impress and I've managed to keep Nelson off the sofa so there are no ginger dog hairs likely to end up in Rob's bowl of chilli. (Ok so maybe I'm a bit paranoid, but it's not like it hasn't happened before.) And just in case, that's why the lamps are placed strategically – not just for romantic reasons. If he does get a ginger dog hair in his food, he won't be able to see it.

I'm going for casual yet sophisticated. Heels (of course) teamed with some dark blue skinny jeans (luckily didn't put any weight on in Saudi – probably due to the lack of alcohol) and fitted sweater with a slight hint of cleavage (in dark red just in case I spill any chilli sauce down my front).

And the icing on the cake? Frankie's promised faithfully she'll be gone by 2030 (and it didn't even cost me anything).

Everything is perfect...

1935 I can see Rob's headlights in the drive and quickly down my glass of wine in an effort to quell my nerves. (It *is* my first...)

I've already given Rob instructions to come around the back of the house and up the stairs to my flat so don't want to look too eager by meeting him at the back door.
I content myself with looking over the banister to make sure that he doesn't go into mum's flat by mistake (I haven't *actually* mentioned that I live above my mother yet...)

I'm aiming to get him into the living room before Frankie comes out of her room opposite so that he doesn't have chance to glimpse the scene of carnage that is her bedroom through the open door. (To be fair, she has had strict instructions not to come out until we're ensconced on the sofa).

I hear the door open downstairs and lean over the railing to attract his attention. Rob glances up and my heart does a little somersault. I have time to notice that he's changed out of his uniform (somewhere from Portsmouth to here?) and is now wearing a pair of jeans and a polo shirt with the logo *'Better a bad day on the water than a good day in the office'*.

I'm not convinced.

I wait for him to reach the top of the stairs and, smiling, he leans forward to give me a light kiss on the lips.

He smells yummy (a change of clothing *and* a shower...?)

Ok, it's Showtime!

2000 We sit together on the sofa. Not so close that you'd have to get a crow bar to prize us apart (wouldn't do to be all over him like a rash) but close enough to touch...

I feel like an anxious teenager and I can tell Rob's a bit nervous too. I've brought him a glass of wine but as he's driving it's not likely to provide him with much in the way of dutch courage.

Still that's not too much of a problem; I think I can manage to drink enough liquid courage for both of us...

He says all the right things about my flat and he makes a nice fuss of Nelson who has now left dog hairs all over his jeans (why did I bother?)

He doesn't seem to care though; however, I decide to shoo Nelson out of the room before he ends up with drool all over his shoes (that's Nelson doing the slobbering obviously – really hoping dribbling is not one of Rob's bad habits.)

I hear the door to Frankie's room open and close and, after a slight pause, she comes into the living room.

My daughter Frankie is gorgeous – but she towers over me by a good 7 inches. As Rob jumps up while I make the introductions, I can see his eyes glance from me back to her a couple of times in slight disbelief.

"Don't worry; I didn't come out this size." Frankie offers cheerfully, relishing his discomfort.

I want to kill her.

Instead I laugh lightly at her 'little joke' and then glare at her as Rob goes to sit down again.

She simply grins back at me, unrepentant – why did I ever think having children would be so rewarding?

Luckily she doesn't linger...

I can hear her moving about in the kitchen as I quickly glance down at my watch and sit back down. I decide to wait until she's gone before re-heating the chilli, just in case Rob decides to follow me in to the kitchen (not ready for extended chat between possible new boyfriend and potentially vulgar but definitely loud daughter).

"ER MUM?" Not only loud but alarmed – even slightly strangled...

I glance over at Rob with a little 'What now' smile (completely contrasting my 'oh f*ck what's happened sick feeling inside...) and get up to head to the kitchen.

Once there, I'm just about to berate my inconsiderate daughter in a loud whisper when I notice what she's pointing at...

OMG Nelson's eaten the chilli.

Well to be fair, not *all* of it, just a substantial portion; enough to leave a massive big hole in the middle of the pan...!

Why oh why did I leave the pan where he could reach it...?

Why oh why did I shoo him out of the living room...?

Why oh why did I make the chilli so early? (At least he would have got a burnt nose for his trouble.)

WHY OH WHY DID I EVEN HAVE A BLOODY DOG IN THE FIRST PLACE.........?

Frankie and I stare at one another in disbelief while Nelson stands wagging his tail uncertainly between us.

"What am I going to do?" My whisper comes out like a strangled squeak. I know that Frankie can see the escalating hysteria in my eyes (I briefly think she's going to slap me across the face in a pre-emptive effort to snap me out of it and I step back as self preservation takes precedence for a couple of seconds...)

Instead she contents herself with shaking my arm and telling me to pull myself together. Briskly she plunges the wooden spoon back into what's left of the chilli mixture and begins stirring it briskly (completely ignoring the fact that Nelson's snout has been stuck inside it – thankfully I don't think he actually licked the spoon – still I suppose that's a moot point really with regards to potential 'dog poisoning'. Mind you, I read somewhere that a dog's saliva is actually antiseptic...)

I hold on to that fact in desperation. If we remove every part of the chilli that Nelson's sampled, there won't be enough left to eat.

On Frankie's direction, I head to the cupboard to grab another tin of baked beans (not keen on kidney beans!) to bulk it up a bit and pretty soon we can't even tell that there's any missing.

Catastrophe averted.

Still I'd better reheat it to a sufficient temperature (like nuclear) to ensure any potential dog bacteria is well and truly dead. After putting it onto a low heat, I grab another (large) glass of wine and make a concerted effort to stroll nonchalantly back into the living room.

I don't even look at Nelson.

The ginger hellhound wisely decides to retreat with Frankie back into her bedroom.

"Is everything ok?" Rob looks a little concerned. Obviously my little 'what now' smile did not completely hide the panic inside.

"Everything's fine. Just a small personal problem with Frankie - daughters you know." I laugh lightly, hoping against hope that Frankie can't hear me.

If she can, I know it will cost me later...

I sit back down on the sofa and he actually takes my hand (the one without the wine glass in it).

For one mad moment I want to throw caution to the winds and plonk myself in his lap but his next words throw a dash of cold water on the whole 'give it to me now' idea (that and the fact that I'm still holding said glass of wine).

"The weather's looking really good for tomorrow."

Now this I am well aware of, having checked the weather forecast on an hourly basis since returning from Saudi.

Latest prediction for the weekend: Cold with sunshine and cloud accompanied by a fairly stiff breeze.

It's the last bit that concerns me. What the hell is a 'fairly stiff breeze? Does that mean it's going to be 'blowing a bloody hooley' in naval speak?

I'm pretty sure that my trepidation is written all over my face which prompts Rob to frown a little before asking hesitantly, "You do want to go sailing tomorrow don't you?"

Ruthlessly forcing down my misgivings, I squeeze his hand and answer firmly, "Of course, I'm really looking forward to it; it'll be a great adventure...

The relief on his face makes it all worthwhile and he smiles broadly before leaning forward and kissing me again. This time a little more thoroughly, giving promises of what's to come.

And all of a sudden, I *am* looking forward to it.

As the kiss finishes, I stare into his eyes and am delighted to note that they are now quite heavy lidded with what I'm hoping is lust and not a need to go to the toilet!

Shit, the chilli...

I jump up (wine still in hand and not a drop spilled...) and excusing myself, I hurry back into the kitchen.

Where the chilli is now bubbling away merrily and developing a nice burnt crust on the bottom.

Damn it. I gingerly help myself to a small spoonful and breathe a sigh of relief. It tastes ok and as long as I don't scrape too far down to the bottom, all should be fine.

Hope he doesn't want seconds though.

I'll make sure I give him plenty of crusty bread...

I pop back into the living to room to check Rob's ready to eat and, at his enthusiastic nod, I tell him to stay where he is (might be coming over a bit bossy but obviously don't want him to spot the burnt bits, especially if I'm going to dazzle him with my, er, ground-breaking cooking skills...)

And besides, I need to put the 'Uncle Ben's' packet of rice in the microwave first.

2300 The evening's been a resounding success though I say so myself. Only one additional little hiccup was when I had to rush to get Rob a drink of water after he took a large mouthful of chilli which I'd forgotten to warn him was boiling hot ....

However, he assured me that it hadn't left any blisters!

He only just left in time to catch the last ferry back to Dartmouth and I could tell he didn't want to go (I didn't want him to go either but as we all know, it doesn't hurt to create a little anticipation...)

The plan is for me to meet him at Dartmouth Marina at 1000 tomorrow. He's going to do all the shopping beforehand.

I'm actually (unbelievably really) beginning to get a little excited about the whole thing.

Although, as he kissed me goodbye, he did gently suggest that I don't wear heels...

Does he think I've got a death wish? The stunted gnome look is definitely preferable to falling overboard.

Saturday 7 November

O800 Ok, everything is packed in my overnight bag and I'm just putting the finishing touches to my 'nautical' ensemble...

I'm wearing navy combat trousers. which I got from Next, not Army and Navy Stores, so not only do they actually fit, but they're quite trendy as well. I've teamed them with a cheerful red sweater, a jaunty red, navy and white scarf around my neck and navy deck shoes. Mind you, looking in the mirror I'm a tad concerned that maybe I've overdone it a bit and now look like an extra from 'The Love Boat' (or even worse 'Flipper'...) But then both TV series did air in the early 70s, and Rob - as he's 10 years younger than me - is not likely to have seen either. Although I suppose he could have seen the re-runs...

I decide to head over to Frankie's room to ask if I look pathetic.

0810 Apparently I look fine – or that's what she said after she'd finished laughing.

I don't know why I bothered asking. Of course I refused to react in response to her immature amusement and opted instead for a dignified exit (after letting Nelson into her bedroom with instructions to dive bomb the bed).

0930 I'm standing at the river's edge in Dart Marina and I'm seriously beginning to think I really have overdone it. All the yachtie types around me are not only dressed in the scruffiest of kit but also look like they haven't washed in a week…

I might as well have 'I've never done this before' tattooed on my forehead.

I sigh. Why couldn't he just have had a gin palace moored in the Med?

0945 I take it back. Rob's boat (sorry yacht) is called Compass Rose and she's lovely. Admittedly, she does have an inordinate number of different coloured ropes that don't seem to be actually attached to anything and appear to have no useful purpose apart from potentially causing all kinds of nasty injuries to anyone attempting to step over them; nevertheless I have made it in one piece down into the 'saloon' where I am now cosily ensconced with a cup of coffee and a packet of ginger nuts (apparently they help to ward off sea sickness and although I feel absolutely fine, it's a great excuse to take another one).

Dunking my biscuit, I look around me with interest. Both the saloon and small kitchen galley are finished in delightful oak panelling with beautiful wooden carvings decorating each corner; there are colourful cushions scattered on the seats and family pictures on the walls (sorry bulkheads) both adding to the cosy atmosphere. I haven't seen the bedroom cabins yet but my imagination is conjuring up a nice double bed (don't mind if it's only a 4ft one) with lovely fluffy pillows and maybe a couple of those round window thingies so that we can lay in each other's arms looking up at the stars…

Can't we just stay here?

1015 The main cabin is not *quite* as expected. First of all the ceiling is so low there is a high risk of me braining myself just in the act of climbing into bed. Secondly, the *top* of the bed might just pass muster as a double (providing we both lie on our sides) but the bottom tapers to about 18 inches wide, at the end of which there is a 'porthole' giving a grand view of 2 pairs of wellies and a spare life buoy.

On the plus side, it will definitely give us the opportunity to get to know each other a little better; however on the minus side, any sexual gymnastics on my part could well end up giving me an impromptu lobotomy...

Still, Rob's enthusiasm is infectious and I do my best to look suitably impressed. Especially when (bless him) he blushingly asks if I would prefer my own cabin (really have to force myself not to ask if he could show it to me before I make a decision...)

1110 We're finally underway. Rob is at the helm after making sure I'm comfortably settled in the cockpit with a blanket and a hot toddy. As I snuggle down into my blanket and sip my drink, I really enjoy taking in the picturesque sights on both sides of the river as we head towards the mouth of the Dart. Things are really looking up. I just know this is going to be so much fun...

1315 I'm never ever again setting foot on any floating vessel smaller than an aircraft carrier.

6 ginger biscuits and 10 pieces of crystallized ginger have failed dismally.

I feel sick. Although, if I'm being honest, it does occur to me that overindulgence of said ginger might actually have worsened the situation.

Rob appears sympathetic but he's busy navigating (and of course I'm truly grateful – wouldn't want to end up in France).

I suggest that I go and lie down in the cabin but Rob assures me that not being able to see the horizon will just make it all the worse. He goes on to promise that it will soon get better.

I resist the urge to respond that it had better if he's looking to see any action that doesn't involve a bucket between the sheets tonight...

1345 Beginning to feel slightly better as promised. Rob asks me if I fancy having a go on the helm so, not wanting to look like a party pooper, I gingerly put aside my snugly blanket and make my way across the cockpit.

Rob guides my hands to the correct position on the wheel and shows me how to look for important things like direction (always a good one) and water depth (duh…)

I'm beginning to enjoy myself. The wind is blowing my hair away from my face and I really do feel like Kate Winslet standing on the bow in 'Titanic' (minus the iceberg – bit too far south for that – aren't we?)

Up to now Rob has been using the engine to power the boat but now he suggests that we (we?) put the sails up. Really not entirely comfortable with this but Rob assures me (he does reassurance very well) that he will take care of the sails while I continue on the helm.

Just point her into the wind he says blithely…

Right!

1420 Really having a great time. For the last half an hour we've been escorted by a pod of dolphins playing and jumping across the bow. It's quite simply the most amazing thing that's ever happened to me.

And we've just finished a lovely picnic lunch courtesy of Marks and Spencer – it's nice to know he hasn't skimped - and we're now skipping along at a pretty fair rate of knots. The dolphins are still with us and it really is very exciting. I can't believe I've never done this before.

Beginning to feel like a pro; first stop South Devon, second stop South America…

1550 Dusk is now beginning to set in as we come towards

the 'picturesque fishing port of Salcombe which sits prettily at the head of the Kingsbridge Estuary' (It says that on the tourist blurb.)

Apparently we can't simply 'sail' Compass Rose into Salcombe harbour as we have to avoid running aground (works for me). So this is the cunning plan...

I man the helm – making sure I point her in to the wind (did I mention I'm practically a pro now?) while Rob pulls down the sails.

Once the sails are down, we can easily motor into the harbour taking care not to venture into the shallow areas There's actually a gadget on the top of the wheel which measures the depth of the water underneath the keel – very useful.

Simple...

1730 I'm lying in the cabin drinking my 2nd glass of wine – it was either keep plying me with drink or stick a bottle of smelling salts under my nose (Rob wisely stuck to the alcohol – good choice, he'd have gotten a deck shoe up his nose if he'd tried to stick anything else near my sinuses...)

I've only just calmed down. It really should have been simple – Rob assures me that it's never happened to him before (he didn't actually *say* that's because he's never had me on board before).

I can't believe that I've narrowly escaped death by drowning, capsizing, shipwrecking – any of those words fit nicely.

Oh and one additional one – being socked in the head by the boom as it swung past my head - at least half a dozen times.

Everything was fine until Rob started to dismantle the sail. There I was doing my 'aye aye sir' at the helm. Rob had just turned the engine for me with instructions to turn her into the wind as soon as the main sail started to drop.

What he didn't tell me was that THE BLOODY ENGINE WAS IN NEUTRAL.

So, as soon as I began turning the wheel towards the wind, a big fat nothing happened.

By this time the sail was coming down and we were heading straight towards a group of rocks sticking out of the water.

And the boom was swinging uncontrollably backwards and forwards at my head (if you don't know what a boom is, think of a big thick pole of wood the size of a telegraph pole...) as Rob fought to control the main sail as it came down.

I'm not ashamed to say I was a tad hysterical, with the words 'rocks' and 'hit' and 'drown' being the main 3 words I was screaming at the top of my lungs.

I have to say that Rob didn't appear to lose his nerve (apart from the fact that he did say – in a very clipped voice – at one point "You're not helping...")

Just as I was about to dive over the side (or step out onto the group of rocks – we really were that close...) Rob had the most amazing idea (bloody amazing to me anyway) to unfurl the small forward sail in an effort to catch the wind.

And just like that... we simply sailed right past the rocks and out of certain death (or at the very least the possibility of being stranded overnight on a very dark and very damp boulder).

That was when he discovered that the engine was in neutral – which is why the boat was not responding to my frantic yanking of the wheel.

How was I to know I had to put it in gear if *he didn't tell me...?*

I'm not a bloody mind reader (well, ok, I didn't actually *say* that – just like he didn't actually *say* it was my fault...)

Probably best to chalk it up to slight miscommunication and have another glass of rosé (mind you I'm sure my blood pressure must have rocketed with all the trauma – perhaps I should be drinking red wine).

1815 2½ glasses of wine later and I'm feeling much more sanguine about the whole episode – in fact I'm actually feeling pretty intrepid (you know a bit like Ellan McArthur when she won that Atlantic race thingy). Plus Rob is being very attentive which is lovely. He's laid out some hors d'oeuvres (M&S again) to tempt my appetite (never really needs much tempting – even in the face of certain death...)

We're moored up on a buoy in the middle of Salcombe harbour and he's booked a table for us in a cosy restaurant on the water front. It's all very romantic – especially as so far it's not raining.

Bloody cold and dark though – not sure about our method of transport to get to said cosy restaurant! Apparently we're being picked up by a 'water taxi' at 1900.

Yep, in this yachty world, there are such things as water taxis – even in November.

Rob asks me if I'd like a shower before we go, and I gape at him for a few seconds having resigned myself to not actually washing at all for these 2 days - thank goodness for grown up baby wipes...

"That'd be lovely." I finally splutter. I wonder what I'm letting myself in for as visions of hand pumping freezing cold water over me spring in to my head.

1830 I really needn't have worried. The shower was actually brilliant. Lovely and hot – some kind of electric pump thing (my eyes glazed over while Rob was trying to explain it to me). As I came out, Rob had stepped up the heater in the saloon and the whole room was completely toasty.

Still, I'm now stood in nothing but a towel and embarrassment is really kicking in...

So, what do I do? I completely wimp out and scuttle into the forward cabin to dress in the 2 foot square space between the door and the bunk.

I doubt Kate Winslet would have been so pathetic. But say what you will, I want my first disrobing to be under (much) lower lighting...

1900 The water taxi arrives promptly and Rob helps me down the ladder and into the tiny cockpit (think he really wanted a feel of my bottom – sort of a bit of heads up as to what to expect later...)

Everything is pretty dark with only the lights from the shore illuminating our ghostly surroundings. I feel a bit like an extra from the Dirty Dozen – all I need is the black face paint. I content myself by gripping Rob's hand tightly and I can just see the outline of his answering smile.

2230 I really don't know where the evening has gone and I've had the most wonderful time. The restaurant was perfect. Very cosy with soft lighting and romantic, intimate booths and absolutely divine food (definitely not worrying about the diet tonight).

We've also consumed the best part of 2 bottles of wine (between us of course) and we're now finally finishing off with liqueur coffees and homemade chocolates.

I fully admit to being more than a little squiffy as well as a tad full. Beginning to think I should have considered possible upcoming bedroom acrobatics before I had the third chocolate mint...

Still, I'm feeling very mellow and relaxed and (real bonus) any nerves about the night ahead have unquestionably disappeared.

Mind you, got the water taxi to negotiate yet – really need to concentrate or I might be undertaking some exercise of the cold wet variety which is definitely not what I had in mind.

2315 Scratch that, the nerves haven't gone at all.

I'm sitting in the saloon while Rob's using the bathroom (hope he doesn't forget to clean his teeth). My stomach's doing back flips. I can't remember the last time I did this (well I can, but really don't want to dwell on it).

I know people say it's like riding a bike – you never forget how to do it; the problem is, so much is expected of 'mature women' nowadays (you know, the whole 'cougar' thing.) We're supposed to be phenomenal in bed. I don't know who started that rumour, but, whoever it was, they want shooting.

Oh God he's finished, think I'm about to have palpitations…

2330 Have just finished in the bathroom and Rob's making us both a coffee (without any alcohol in it). He seems really relaxed about the whole thing which is making me feel a little better, although I can't help wondering how many times *he's* done this recently. Still he's sensitive enough not to just drag me to bed - even though that might have had its advantages…)

I'm wearing my 'special occasion' silk dressing gown (ok it's pretty much a negligee but not *quite* Ann Somers…) and Rob's wearing a large rugby shirt and a pair of boxers (thank God he doesn't wear budgie smugglers).

He looks pretty sexy actually – nerves definitely beginning to wane.

We finish drinking our coffee and Rob casually puts his arm around my shoulders as he leans in for a kiss.

5 minutes later and I'm tingly all over. I wonder how he's going to maneuver us from the saloon to the bedroom, but in the end he simply cups my face in his hands and asks if I'd like to go to

bed.

Really think I might be falling in love...

Sunday 8 November

O835 I slowly come awake to the realization that I'm lying snugly next to a warm male body and it feels simply wonderful, apart from the fact that my right arm has gone to sleep which is what woke me in the first place.

Rob is still snoring softly in my left ear and as I quietly and carefully shift my trapped arm, my thoughts inevitably drift back to last night.

Mm, it was lovely. There were a couple of potentially embarrassing moments, first off when we actually climbed into bed (the only way in is by clambering over the pillows at the head of the bunk) and, as the ceiling is not actually high enough to sit up properly, I got all caught up in the hem of my negligee and nearly strangled myself before managing to yank the bloody thing off my shoulder (definitely won't go down as one of the sexiest disrobings in history). Subsequently, even more embarrassing, when I did the whole 'dominant cougary' thing by climbing on top, I discovered that you really do need more than a 3 foot headroom to get a bit of leverage and banging ones head with a resounding crack on said ultra low ceiling does nothing to promote an 'amazing in bed' reputation (luckily I didn't actually pass out and collapse on top of him so was able to hide just how much it hurt – and of course the darkness hid the tears of pain...)

Afterwards, naturally I'd forgotten just how awkward that post coital moment can be – especially when climbing out of bed is more precarious than getting into it. We did manage to avoid kicking each other in the head though which I think definitely augers well for a lasting relationship.

I feel gingerly to see if there's a lump on the top of my head and as I turn my head experimentally from side to side, I come face to face with Rob's sleepy but smiling face. I have time to register that he really does have the loveliest blue eyes before he pulls me to him and I forget banged heads and everything else for a little while...

0905 Rob's got out of bed to make me a cup of tea and to put on the heater. I snuggle down into the duvet, enjoying the feeling of space for a little while (cosy is all well and good but the necessary bedroom contortions are definitely taking a toll on this particular cougar).

I can hear Rob moving about in the galley and I reflect that the experiences of last night and this morning have truly moved us way beyond the normal 'first time' tensions - especially having Rob's dangly bits briefly hanging over my head as he struggled out of the bunk!

I laugh quietly to myself and realize that I haven't had so much fun in ages...

1530 There were no dolphins on the way back (but no near misses either). Rob patiently explained the uses of the different coloured ropes to me but refrained from suggesting we put up the sails again (sensible man).

I've truly had the most amazing couple of days and as I follow Rob onto the jetty at BRNC, I want to sing and shout like a teenager. However, I content myself with grinning like an idiot and gripping Rob's hand tightly as he tows me up the hill towards the College.

We're going to his cabin for a coffee and to grab his gear before heading back to my flat for the rest of the evening (and the night...)

I can't remember the last time I was so happy.

1550 I have to admit that I'm puffing a bit by the time we arrive at the corridor leading to Rob's cabin and so I'm a few yards behind him as he pushes open the door. I just have time to wonder why it's not locked when I see him stop abruptly and then push the door open further before stepping through and allowing it to shut behind him.

Frowning, I sense that something's wrong and hurry to catch up. As I reach the door to his cabin I can hear voices and feel an unexpected sensation of dread in the pit of my stomach.

Heart thumping I push open the door to see Rob standing with his arms on the waist of a strange woman. Her arms are linked around his neck and they are kissing.

Call me intuitive but I don't think this is his sister.
As I stand staring stupidly, Rob abruptly pulls away and disentangles himself before turning towards me with an anguished look on his face.

He seems at a complete loss as to what to do and I have time to register that the woman can't be much older than her early twenties before she steps forward and, taking matters into her own hands, introduces herself.

"Hi I'm Tracy, Rob's girlfriend. So Rob's just taken you for a sail on his yacht. How cute! Rather you than me; Rob knows I prefer to stick to the kind of boat that sports a full length Olympic swimming pool"

I feel sick. My breath whooshes out of me like I've just been kicked in the ribs.

Oh my God, I've been such an idiot.

2330   I'm well and truly drunk.   Not just squiffy but unequivocally, not to mention blindly, drunk.

I couldn't tell you how I got home. I remember standing in Rob's cabin like a complete imbecile with my mouth open looking from one to the other. I recall actually thinking for a couple of seconds that she was making some kind of joke and waiting for the punch line.

Instead there was this awful silence. I was sure they could both hear the thudding of my heart, it sounded so loud in my ears. As Rob stepped forward and tried to speak, I made a strangled noise and put out my hand to wave him back.

Somehow I pulled myself together and began backing towards the cabin door. I almost didn't recognize my voice when I finally managed to speak.

"Er yes, absolutely. Well, thanks for the sailing lesson Rob, we must do it again sometime."

I don't know what happened next, I think I simply turned and fled the room.

I can't remember getting back to my car or the subsequent journey home. Luckily there was no one in when I arrived back at the flat. Just Nelson.

I sat and cried for an hour while Nelson did his best to climb onto my knee. Then I did what every woman does who finds out that the man she's fallen in love with is a complete and utter rat.

I opened a bottle.

Week 10

Monday 9 November

O815 I've locked the office door and posted a sign on it saying 'Do not disturb'. My excuse is that I'm putting together my report on the Saudi trip.

In reality I'm sitting staring at a blank computer screen nursing a cold cup of coffee and feeling like absolute crap. I'm horribly hung over and just want to curl up in bed for the next year and tell the world to go f*ck itself.

Why oh why did I let myself fall for this man. I'm so stupid, so completely and utterly stupid. It's not like I can't remember this pain. I've been here before and I swore I would never *ever* put myself in this position again. And yet here I am. How and when did love creep in to the equation?

How could I have got it so wrong?

Again…

Nelson is sitting at my feet and as he rests his head on my toes with a mournful sigh, I feel the tears starting again.

I want to pull myself together, I really do, but it just hurts so much.

I wonder if there's any way I can hole up in my office for the rest of the term. If I can just get to Christmas leave without seeing Rob, I think I'll be ok.

I console myself with the fact that no one knows what's happened because hardly anyone knew we'd started dating. There'll be no pitying looks at least…

1030 Still staring at the computer. I can hear the students clambering down the stairs for stand easy. I don't move.

1230 Still staring at the computer. I'm vaguely aware that it's lunch time but the thought of food makes me want to throw up.

Nelson's given up on me and retreated to his chair (of course he's a bloody man).

Suddenly my phone pings with a text message.

It's Rob

My heart begins thumping erratically and I'm tempted to simply delete it without reading but despite everything, pathetically, I still want to believe that there's been some kind of horrible mix up.

Heart pounding, I open the message…

Bev. I'm so sorry 4 what happened yesterday. Been trying to pluck up the courage all morning to call u but didn't know what to say. Had no idea Tracy would be in my cabin, really thought it was over between us. Can u please give me some time to sort myself out?

For a second I actually think I'm going to be sick. My head is now throbbing in time with my heart. What do I say? Do I hang on to the few pitiful crumbs he's tossed at me? Sit here and wait just in case it doesn't work out again with his bimbo girlfriend?

I close my eyes and take a deep breath and then begin texting back…

No worries Rob. We had fun but it was nothing serious. Hope all goes well between u & Tracy

I just can't do it all over again. I simply can't.

I press send.

Friday 13 November

1 615 Have managed to avoid Rob all week – which to be fair hasn't been all that difficult given that I've not actually left my office except to go home.

Since replying to Rob's text, I've gone from staring at a blank computer screen, to throwing myself into my work which has helped keep the demons away during the day and of course, I've finished the Saudi report in record time (nothing like a spot of heartache to make a person focus on, well, anything, to keep the misery at bay).

And, if I've been drinking far too much in the evenings, Rosie and Frankie have been wise enough not to say anything.

The teachers just think I've been too busy to hold a staff meeting but that's something I can't put off for much longer. I'll need to hold a meeting on Monday to discuss the final 4 weeks leading up to the end of term language tests.

Which is another way of taking my mind off the mess that is my love life.

Sarah's been calling me all week. She knows something's wrong, especially when I made an excuse to avoid Shareholders yesterday (after a whole week away – think she's convinced an alien has inhabited my body).

She finally came up to my office this morning and made me promise to have a pre-ferry drink with her down at the Cherub.

She had a very determined look on her face which doesn't bode well for my determination not to talk about it. What she doesn't realise is that the way I'm feeling, she may well be driving me home afterwards…

1900 Actually feel a little better. Stuck to one glass of wine (ok it was a large but give me a break) and although I tried to make light of what had happened, she could tell that the whole thing has affected me badly.

By the time we left, she'd decided that we would be attending every social function taking place in the College in the lead up to Christmas, including 'Dine Leavers' in Week 12; the Cocktail Parties in Week 13 and culminating in the Christmas Ball at the end of Week 14. My protestations fell on deaf ears. I think 'F*ck Him' was the term she used.

In the end it was easier to agree than to continue arguing. Maybe my enthusiasm will pick up once I've had another few glasses of wine this evening.

I smother the little warning voice in the back of my mind that tells me I'm drinking too much.

At the moment it's dulling the pain and that's all I can deal with right now.

Week 11

Monday 16 November

O700 In the office early this morning – couldn't sleep so thought I might as well come to work.

Don't think Nelson's very impressed with my miserable face, my nocturnal rambles or my early starts; the clue being that he's starting to camp outside my mum's flat.

Bloody traitor! Still I can't really blame him; even I'm pretty pissed off with looking at my face.

I went to the Boathouse yesterday with Jackie, Rosie, Frankie and James. Think maybe they're pretty pissed off too.

1030 Sarah's determined to get me down to the Wardroom for Stand Easy but I'm equally determined not to go. I promise her faithfully I'll go tomorrow.
I know I've got to see him sometime. Just can't face it today.

God I'm such a wimp!

1645 It's time for our long overdue staff meeting. Not only do I owe it to my hard working staff to give them a heads up about the possibility of 60 plus Saudi teenagers darkening our classrooms next summer but I also need an update about our current crop of linguistically challenged cadets...

Plus of course we have to chat about our proposed brand new all singing all dancing Military Language Course.... (Wouldn't want to think that all my suffering on Dartmoor was for nothing.)

1750 Actually feeling much better. We're on track to push through about 70% of our Internationals which I am very relieved about (it's pretty much a miracle actually).

Of course HRH is highly unlikely to be one of them (I'm actually more likely to win the lottery...) Still, his Embassy, and subsequently his father – I hope - are aware of the situation and are happy (relative term) for him to stay in language training for another 14 weeks.
Our MLT (Military Language Course) is coming along nicely, and, last but not least, the teachers actually seemed really pleased about the proposed Saudi Summer School (so naïve...)

Can't think why I didn't remember how much better it is to focus on work rather than romance. From now on I'm determined to concentrate totally on being a professional woman of the world.

Tuesday 17 November

1 105 Took the plunge and went to the Wardroom for Stand Easy. No Rob thank goodness.

Wednesday 18 November

1 115 Sarah dragged me down to Stand Easy again and still no sign of Rob.

Beginning to relax a little.

Thursday 19 November

1025 Shareholders! I know I've got to do it but I've decided to wait a bit and walk in when it's pretty crowded. Then, if Rob's already on the Quarterdeck, I can retreat without being noticed. If he isn't, I'm less likely to be noticed if he does come in.

Good plan...

I know I'm looking good (mainly because I spent an hour making sure of it this morning). A bit pale (but that's always interesting). And, the one good thing to come out of all this, I've actually lost a few more pounds (drinking but not really eating – not a good long term strategy I know).

I can do this – Eat your heart out Rob the Rat...

1105 Beginning to think Rob's actually fallen off the face of the earth. Wanted to pluck up the courage to ask Sam where he was but bottled out at the last minute.

Am now battling images of him cosily ensconced in his cabin with 'Tracy'. Perhaps he's taken the week off to be with her... Maybe she's been staying with him since Sunday? Oh God, even worse, now I've got images of them in bed together.

I chant PWOW to myself as I head back up the language school stairs (short for professional woman of the world – it's easier just to chant the acronym when I'm feeling low. Pause. I've definitely been here too long...)

Roll on end of term!

Week 12

Monday 23 November

1615 I'm sitting in my office waiting for the lessons to finish so that I can swan in and give a little pep talk to those students in the 30% 'underachieving' category (most of them are Qatar Coastguard – no surprise there). I've also got to break the news to them that their Military Attaché is venturing down in to the wilds of Dartmouth on Wednesday in an effort to rally his troops so to speak and encourage them to try a bit harder. I'm not sure what threats he's likely to be using but he's definitely left it a bit late – sort of shutting the gate after the horse has bolted as it were. I've never met Captain Al Baker but have been assured by Rashid at the Qatar Embassy that he is 'very good man'.

Technically I should be working on what 'encouraging' words to say, but in reality I'm actually trying to come up with excuses not to go to Dine Leavers on Thursday. Sarah has put my name down and issued various threats if I chicken out…

Dine Leavers happens once a term and is the opportunity for all members of the Wardroom to get together to say goodbye to those leaving at the end of the term. It usually consists of a Mess Dinner followed by outrageous (and very often false) dits concerning the unfortunate individuals leaving. (Not actually attending the dinner doesn't spare you from being laughed at.) The speech usually falls to the Commander of the College in his capacity as WR president. Of course the proverbial 'dirt' is fed to him from fellow officers who very rarely take any prisoners..

I'm actually only still working here because I daren't leave...

Sarah's told me she has it on good authority that Rob's not intending to come.

I don't ask where he is or who's told her.

I don't want to know.

1645 Feel a bit like Queen Elizabeth I of England when she was rallying the troops at Tilbury prior to the Invasion of the Spanish Armada in 1588. (The history of this place is definitely going to my head.)

Hope she got a better response from her troops than I have with mine.

So, enough with the encouragement, now it's on to the threats...

1700 The thought of their MA coming to see them definitely caused the Qataris to sit up a bit and look a trifle alarmed, which made me wonder what Rashid's definition of 'very good man' actually meant. In fact I thought a couple of them were going to burst in to tears.

None of them attempted to appeal to my better nature though – perhaps they've learned more than I thought...

As I watched them troop down the corridor, I did notice that they were actually a little more regimented and, more amazingly, their uniforms were definitely fitting better (think John's put a stop to the late night takeaways).

So it's not all bad...

1730 Am in the ferry queue and my thoughts inevitably turn to Rob. Feeling pretty low. I haven't even got the heart to risk life and limb preventing a car from jumping into the queue directly in front of me.

The whole thing just makes me so sad. I really thought I'd finally met someone I could truly spend the rest of my life with.

I shouldn't have allowed myself fall for him so quickly. I should have guarded my heart and simply followed my head, making sure I held myself back like every other time since my divorce.

Maybe I've just been too long on my own.

The queue begins moving. I put the car in gear and sigh, just as Nelson leans forward from the backseat and rubs his cold nose on the side of my neck.

Much better to stick to a dog.

Wednesday 25 November

O830 Made an effort to look extra smart today in preparation for the Qatar Military Attaché arriving at 1130. I haven't brought Nelson in to work having learned the hard way that ginger dog hairs and Embassy Ambassadors are not a good mix.

I am hosting Captain Al Baker for lunch in the Wardroom along with Commander NTE (sorry Steve!) which I'm dreading for a couple of reasons:

1. Don't want to see Rob.

2. Don't want Rob to see me.

I know that we're bound to bump into one another eventually. Just don't want it to be during a high profile foreign visit.

1115 John will bring the Captain up to my office as soon as we've been notified of his arrival. We'll have coffee and biscuits in here whilst discussing the small 'problems' we're having with a few of his cadets before he meets with the condemned few to administer his beating (sorry, pep talk).

I've been to the Naafi to pick up a decent packet of biscuits and now I'm left waiting in my office twiddling my thumbs...

1145 John has been alerted by the main gate that our guest has arrived and so I spend the next few minutes checking my appearance, fumigating the office and de-hairing Nelson's chair…

Mind you, think I might have overdone the air freshener.

1155 I can hear John's voice as he comes up the stairs along with a much deeper tone answering him in (very attractive) broken English.

John knocks briefly on my door before pushing it open and gesturing behind him to my (as yet unseen) guest.
Captain Al Baker murmurs his thanks and steps past John and into the room.

Bloody hell. He's absolutely gorgeous…

Think Johnny Depp with a slightly darker complexion and an Omar Sharif accent.

In uniform…

For a few seconds, I'm completely unaware that I'm gaping at him with my mouth open.

Luckily, John comes to the rescue by coughing slightly and making the introductions. Unfortunately I can feel my face begin to flame as I step forward to shake hands.
"Please, take a seat." I'm relieved to note that my voice sounds reasonably normal.

"Thank you," He responds, seating himself in Nelson's chair and glancing round. "I was told you have a dog."

Oh God, can he smell dog? I resolve to give Nelson a bath the moment I get home…

"Er, yes I have but I erm haven't brought him in today."

"Ah, what a shame, I've heard such interesting things about him and I was hoping to meet him in person so to speak."

His smile reveals a row of beautiful white teeth and, as I stare helplessly at the immaculately presented Adonis sitting in his chair, I can only give silent thanks that Nelson isn't here...

As the silence lengthens, John gives me a puzzled look and asks the Captain if he'd like coffee or tea.

What on earth is wrong with me? Anyone would think I've never seen a handsome man before...

As John goes off to make coffee I make a concerted effort to pull myself together, determined to focus on the purpose of the Captain's visit.

Mind you, at least he's taking my mind off Rob...

1225 I've finally begun to relax. Despite his superstar looks, Captain Al Baker (call me Salim) really does appear to be 'very good man'. He shows concern as well as empathy for his struggling cadets – traits which are not always a given in the higher ranks. As our discussion draws to a close, I ask John to go and gather the 'problem' cadets together into an empty classroom.

It's my intention to leave them to it and collect the Captain for lunch shortly before 1300. Which gives me enough time to freshen up my make-up just in case Rob *is* in the Wardroom...

At the very least I can look good.

As I start to rise from my chair, the Captain asks me if I've ever been to Qatar.

Shaking my head with a smile, I sit back down.
"You will love it," He continues leaning forward in his chair. "I am returning home next year – I will love to show you around..."

Assuming that his use of 'will' rather than 'would' is due to a grammatical mistake as opposed to a prediction, I smile politely before saying, "Thank you Salim. If I come to Qatar, that would be lovely, and very kind of you.

He leans forward and I instinctively do the same. Then, in a low intense voice he says passionately, "Come to my country Miss Beverley, I will look after you."

We stare at one another for a second as I wrestle with what I've just heard.

Is he making me a proposition? I open my mouth, just about to inform him that despite what he may have been told, keeping Military Attachés happy is not in the 'Head of English Language' job description...

"My wife will look after you; my children will look after you; my whole family will look after you..."

I shut my mouth again with a mixture of relief and maybe, if I'm honest, a little bit of disappointment. Both dwarfed by overwhelming gratitude that I hadn't actually spoken the words on the tip of my tongue out loud...

As I show the Captain to his cadets, I shudder inwardly at the possible ramifications of that particular misunderstanding. Still, might have to find an excuse to visit the Embassy in London...

Thursday 26 November

1100 Really can't get on with anything. Absolutely dreading tonight in case Rob turns up. We still haven't seen each other since the fateful Sunday and my imagination has since gone in to overdrive (had him married and off on his honeymoon this morning).

All confidence gained from receiving a gorgeous man's attention yesterday seems to have disappeared out of the window and haven't got Nelson here to help me feel loved and needed…

Really, really hoping he doesn't go tonight (Rob that is, not Nelson!)

1700 Have spent most of the day pacing my office. It's Sarah's turn to bring the pre-dinner bottle of wine otherwise I might have been tempted to start already.

Have got to get a grip (PWOW…)

1830 I'm standing in front of the mirror and have to say I think I look really good. My customary red lipstick has taken away some of my pallor and I'm wearing my trusty long black taffeta skirt with a black and white corset – think 18th century courtesan (the only thing I'm missing is a stuck on beauty patch).

I don't usually go quite so over the top, but needs must…

Black heels and long black vintage earrings complete the look.

I answer the door to Sarah and she actually whistles bless her.

Feeling much better than earlier...

1945 Can't help myself, I keep glancing towards the door. I've checked the seating plan that's been pinned on the wall and, horror of horrors, Rob's name is on it.

The only good thing is he's not seated anywhere near me.

And he hasn't arrived yet so maybe he's changed his mind...

1950 The gong rings a 5 minute warning for dinner, giving everyone a chance to 'ease springs' before we sit down.

I'm beginning to think that Rob's not coming and I breathe a sigh of relief as I follow Sarah out of the Wardroom for a quick trip to the heads....

...only to run directly into my nemesis striding towards the Wardroom. My heart slams violently in my chest. He looks gorgeous in his Mess Undress and the bastard doesn't even falter as he sees me. He simply nods to both of us and continues past to the bar.

I want to sit down in the middle of the floor and cry – professional woman of the world be damned.

I glance towards Sarah as she takes my arm sympathetically and I can feel a huge lump come into my throat as the tears threaten my mascara. Oh God I can't cry, not now.

"You ok?" Sarah's concern is nearly my undoing.

"Just need the loo." I manage in a strangled voice.

Once seated in the toilet cubicle, I rest my head in my hands and force myself to simply breathe deeply, trying to quell the impending flood.

My mind once again pictures his face as he walked towards me.

How could he have looked so cold?

Like he really didn't give a damn.

Do I really know him at all?

Sarah knocks lightly on the door. I'm tempted to tell her to go on without me, but I'm damned if I'll let the cheating swine know how much he's hurt me. I take another deep breath and finish off (wouldn't want the time to be wasted totally – there's still a few hours at the table to go...)

"I'm fine." I tell her as I come out of the toilet. Then, determinedly ignoring her doubtful expression, I reapply my lipstick and sweep out of the heads with my best tried and tested 'I don't give a damn' impression.

2005 The Wardroom dining room looks stunning. The tables have been lined up together in a U shape with the Commander seated at the centre of the top table. As always the tables are beautifully laid out with white cloths and the best silver. A myriad of candles cast a warming glow over the whole room and create an alternate world of flickering and dancing shadows in the floor to ceiling windows.

I breathe a sigh of relief as I finally sit down. I know roughly where Rob is sitting but I can't actually see him once I'm seated at the table unless I lean forward. I'm sitting next to Sam on the one side and a Lt Bond on the other (that's his name - really. Bet he can't wait until he gets to Cdr. Mind you, his first name isn't James, it's Adam – feel a bit cheated actually...)

Anyway I'm determined to enjoy myself, and after a couple more glasses of wine, I'm at my sparkling best.
If my sparkling best is a little brittle, only my mum would be able to tell...

2230 Even in my slightly inebriated state, I manage to refrain from overindulging in the port as it comes round the table for the third time, although the same can't be said of my dinner companions! Not sure how long either of them will last in the post dinner shenanigans...

I've only made eye contact with Rob once throughout the evening as I leant forward to listen to someone on the other side of the table. Glancing to the right, I caught Rob's gaze briefly but he looked away before I could discern his expression.

I so wish it really had been simply a bit of fun. My head is beginning to spin a little (although it has to be said it's taking the pressure of my usual bladder inadequacies).

As soon as the speeches are over, I think I'll be calling it a night...

2345 There are 12 leavers all together this term and none of them escaped unscathed. In fact I couldn't help squirming for one poor chap who had apparently conducted an illicit liaison with another officer (female fortunately at least) and was in the habit of sending risqué emails to her which she very obviously enjoyed replying to. As he handed over his post to his replacement, he believed that he'd wiped all the incriminating evidence off his computer's hard drive.

Unfortunately not so.

The emails were read out word for word to the delight of everyone in the room apart from two...

Friday 27 November

O 230 Am lying in bed and I can't sleep. The cabin is absolutely freezing and I stupidly didn't bring my winceyette pyjamas (I've slept in these cabins enough times that I should have known better – they're either boiling hot or bloody arctic).

Of course that's not the only reason I'm tossing and turning. Although I have to say that the rest of the evening did actually turn out to be a bit of an eye opener...

Once the speeches were over, we retired to the Wardroom bar and I fully intended to head straight back to my cabin. But then I saw Rob leave with his mobile phone plastered to his ear and decided to have another drink instead.

Not sure whether I made the right decision, but at least what followed took my mind off my problems for a little while...

After copious amounts of alcohol, officers in the Royal Navy have a proclivity to take part in stunts that might seem to us mere mortals as bizarre and sometimes downright dangerous (in this instant the danger was more about potential frost bite on exposed extremities...)
I am referring to the unanimous (well nearly –the small female contingent weren't so keen) decision to take part in a 'naked ramp race'.

You may well ask...

The ramps in question are the raised walkways surrounding the Parade Ground.

It was decided (really not sure who originally came up with the idea) that all the officers present would take off all their clothes and race around said ramps in their birthday suits.

It was minus 3 outside…

There were predictably no female participants.

So there we were, standing on the porch outside the Wardroom watching 20 grown men run around in the pitch black freezing cold with nothing on but a pair of socks!

Of course Sarah and I made sure we had front row seats – after all, it's not often one gets to see the Commander of the College in all his glory.

I can only reiterate, it really was a very cold night…

0815 Finally gave up trying to sleep at 07.30 (I succumbed to wearing my coat in bed at about 4ish) and decided to get an early start in the office.

Cue sitting in front of my computer, looking at a blank screen.

I know this has got to stop. I'm not some little wimp of a female (well ok, I am fairly little) who needs a man to make her happy. I sit up straighter (PWOW style) and resolve that I am no longer going to keep using alcohol as a crutch…

However, before taking such forthright action, I think I should indulge in one last evening of debauchery this weekend and paint the town red (well pink maybe – we are talking about Torquay).

And what's more, I'm not going to give the 2 timing moron one more thought.
Won't do it tonight though – think I'd better get over this

hangover first.

Sunday 29 November

1035 Am still in bed. I'm never drinking again (well, definitely not in Torquay anyway).

Jackie accompanied me on said rampage of debauchery and Frankie put me to bed when I finally got home, (think I remember her muttering something about this being the wrong way round...)

Also think Nelson actually spent the whole night in my bed with me.

I turn over on to my side and we stare at each other eye to eye...

At least I do actually get to wake up next to the man in my life. And you know what, I'd much rather wake up next to Nelson than some stranger - although, to be fair, my definition of debauchery may be relatively tame compared to some.

Mind you, I suppose there is the advantage that most men would actually be able take themselves off for a wee without me needing to drag myself out of bed to open the door for them (that's the theory...)

In truth, last night was fun (what I can remember of it anyway). And I really did need to get away from the College (and uniformed men in general) for a while. Sort of getting back to basics which is very easy to do in Torquay.

As far as I remember, my embarrassment was confined to taking part in a karaoke duet singing the theme tune from Dirty Dancing. Not really sure if my singing partner (a carpet fitter from Glasgow – call me Rory - at least that's what I think he said – see what I mean about basics?) tried to throw me over his head a la Patrick Swayze but I really wasn't that drunk – although thinking about it, my bottom does feel a bit tender this morning...

Then Jackie and I capped it off with a duet of 'My Way'.
We didn't quite empty the pub (and anyway it was pretty near to closing time).

Think I'll spend the rest of the day in bed...

Week 13

Monday 30 November

1030 The end of term is finally looming and I've got a crazily busy week ahead.

I normally love this part of the term. Everyone is starting to get into a festive mood. The cadets are getting ready to finish their training which culminates in their Passing Out Parade on Thursday of Week 14 (bloody hell, next week). That's followed by the Christmas Ball on the Friday and leave after that (well that is, the holidays start for everyone in uniform – us civvies are here until Christmas Eve).

This year of course, I've got lots of additional responsibilities (not to mention a broken heart – just in case you've forgotten...)

And then there are the Squadron Cocktail Parties on Wednesday evening. They're a 'Black Box' event - meaning that every Wardroom member has to attend on pain of death, or at the very least a public dressing down by the Commander – mind you, it has to be said he doesn't seem quite so intimidating after Dine Leavers...)
Yet another opportunity to come face to face with Rob.

Oh joy.

But I *am* beginning to feel better and so I've decided not to stop on board overnight. I've drunk enough to sink a battleship over the last couple of weeks and, as I've already decided, I'm not going to become a sad middle aged woman who takes refuge in a bottle of wine every night to alleviate her loneliness. Anyway, I drink wine with my mum – so I'm not *technically* alone…

It will also give me an excuse to leave fairly early – the constant late nights are beginning to catch up and I've not even started my Christmas shopping (even thinking about it makes me hyperventilate). Still, at least it's Jackie's turn to cook Christmas dinner this year.

Think Nelson needs some sugar!

1530 I feel completely drained. I've just come out of the College Assessment Group (known as the CAG strangely enough…) This is where the fate of the soon to Pass Out cadets is finally decided. My job is to report the status of the International cadets in English Language Training. It's all very intimidating and I really don't enjoy it (definitely not one of the perks of being a PWOW).

And this time Rob was there in his capacity as VSO. (How could I have forgotten?)

So, finally, absolutely no way to avoid speaking with him…

Not sure I handled myself particularly well. He just seemed so intimidating. Obviously he took great pains not to show this side of himself when trying to get into my pants. (Ok, a little voice is telling me I'm being slightly unfair, not to mention bitchy. He's a professional and just because *I'm* struggling to handle the whole thing…)

And to be honest, it doesn't make me want him any the less – unfortunately! His authoritative, clipped manner gave an aura of leadership that I hadn't seen in Rob before.

Another side to him that I so wish I had a future to explore.

Maybe I'll start cutting down on the wine tomorrow night…

Tuesday 1 December

1 630 Just come out of a final staff meeting before the end of term assessments start tomorrow.

This is it. This is what the whole term has been about...

Perhaps I will just have *one* glass tonight.

Wednesday 2 December

1 105 Just come back from Stand Easy. They're putting up giant Christmas trees in the Wardroom, Senior Gunroom and the Quarterdeck in preparation for the cocktail parties tonight. It all seems too early really, but that could just be because I don't feel in a particularly festive mood.

The Language school is quiet as all the students are doing their writing tests elsewhere in the College.

I wander into one of the classrooms to stare out of the window. The last time I did this was at the start of the term.

The sun was shining over the River Dart and I was so happy and excited.

What a difference a few short weeks can make. There's no sun to be seen now; the clouds seem scarcely higher than the College clock tower and are iron grey with impending rain. The Parade Ground below is filled with cadets shivering with cold as they rehearse for the Passing Out Parade, now only a week away.

Turning away, I head back into my office where Nelson is sprawled out in customary abandonment on his chair.

His loud snores pierce both the silence and my gloom.
In fact I suddenly find that I'm actually looking forward to this evening. Yet another training evolution in the RN school of etiquette; this is the opportunity for those cadets passing out to show off their newly developed conversational skills to their

friends and families. St Vincent squadron will be hosting on the Quarterdeck and Cunningham squadron in the Senior Gun Room.

Think I'll probably make an effort to spend most of my time in the SGR...

1845 As I'm not stopping overnight, I intend to get changed in my office, but first of all, I take Nelson out for a quick jaunt. Most of the teachers have stayed behind to attend and there's a bustling festive atmosphere permeating the school as I get back.

I hurriedly change into a fitted black velvet square necked dress. The neck is low, but not too much so and the hem sits just shy of the floor, making it perfect for this sort of occasion. Then I quickly reapply my make-up, forsaking my trademark red lipstick for a more restrained and less formal pale pink. Black satin court shoes complete the outfit and, after a quick fluff of my hair, I'm ready to roll.

After giving Nelson his dinner, I take a moment and stand looking at myself in the full length mirror that graces my office wall. I can't help but smile a little ruefully - I actually look pretty good. Except for the whole pain bit, I think heartbreak suits me...

2100 I have so far avoided the Quarterdeck and Sarah has loyally stayed with me but I know it's only fair to give her the opportunity to 'do' St Vincent squadron (in the very broadest sense of course). It's a big room and I shouldn't have any difficulty avoiding Rob – as the Senior Squadron Officer he'll have his hands full anyway.

I follow her hesitantly down The Corridor and onto the Quarterdeck where we're instantly surrounded by cadets offering to fetch us another drink. (It has to be said, they do take their hosting role very seriously). I opt for an orange juice having already consumed my alcohol allowance for this evening (beginning to wish I'd elected to stay on board...) Still, I can see that Rob is tied up on the other side of the room and even without the assistance of some liquid courage, I finally allow myself to relax.

Staring down into my drink, I listen and simply let the conversation flow over and around me.

Which turns out to be a monumental mistake, as I suddenly hear his voice. And it's not from the other side of the room...

Startled, I look up, straight into blue eyes that are only feet away. My heart thuds painfully and all calmness dissipates instantly.

"Hello Sir, can we get you another drink?" The cadets fall over themselves to accommodate their VSO who is now standing directly in front of me. I realise with panic that Sarah has drifted away slightly and is now laughing with group of officers and too far-off for me to garner any support from that direction.

How the hell did he get from there to here so bloody quickly? Helplessly I stand and stare at him. I simply don't know what to say (is that a first?)

Sensing the subtle tension, the cadets begin drifting away with various excuses and I resist the urge to grab hold of the one next to me and beg him to stay...

All too soon we're left alone and the silence starts to become painful. He is still staring at me, eyes intent and unreadable.

In the end, as always, I break first and coughing slightly I ask him whether he's enjoying the evening. I hate the stilted sound of my voice and I can't help but remember lying with him warm and naked in the cabin on Compass Rose.

I close my eyes and just want to cry...

His answer when it comes is vague and non-committal, revealing nothing of his feelings.

"How about you. Are you having a good time?" I can tell he

doesn't want to talk to me; his question is polite, nothing more.

I glance towards Sarah desperately hoping that she'll come over and rescue me but her back is turned towards me and she has no idea I'm in trouble.

Suddenly I snap and determine to put an end to this farce.

"I'm having a lovely evening thank you Rob." I offer with false cheerfulness. "Are you looking forward to the holidays? Spending Christmas with Tracy?"

I could bite out my tongue. I didn't mean to say her name, really I didn't.

He stares back at me and, for a second I think he's not going to answer.

"I'm looking forward to seeing my son Jack over Christmas. I have no idea what Tracy's doing; I haven't seen her since the Sunday before last. If you'll excuse me please."

Then he walks away, just like that.

And for the second time in as many minutes I'm completely speechless...

2230 I'm sitting in the car waiting for the last ferry to Paignton. The darkness is pretty frigid without the engine on but I hardly notice as my mind replays his words to me over and over again.

He hasn't seen her since that day.

I frantically think back to the text Rob sent me the day after.

He asked me to give him some time to sort himself out.

He didn't say he was *still* with his bimbo girlfriend. In fact he said he thought it was finished.

He asked me to give him time...

And what did I do? I told him to get lost. I made an assumption

255

without ever giving him time to explain himself.

I'm stone cold sober, and for the first time in 2 weeks I actually face the fact that I had reacted without thinking – based on a belief that was pure conjecture...

What do they say? Assumption is the mother of all f*ckups...

And it looks like I might have I f*cked up – royally!

Thursday 3 December

0830 I haven't slept a wink all night – what a surprise.

And the result of all those sleepless hours? (Apart from the fact that my eyes feel like they've got boulders in them, never mind grit.) I came to following conclusions.

1. I'm in love with Rob
2. He's not a cheating moron.
3. I've absolutely no idea how to get him to give me a second chance.

1635 I've spent most of the day marking the students' writing tests which usually give rise to a few snickers if not downright hilarity.

Today however, not even HRH's classic sentence 'Ben is on the bich' (as opposed to 'beach' rather than 'bitch) failed to elicit so much as a titter.

I really don't know what to do.

I keep seeing Rob's face as he walked away from me on the Quarterdeck. I don't think he's going to listen to whatever I have to say.

I toy with the idea of 'accidentally' bumping in to him – maybe I could engineer a fall at his feet on The Corridor (very easily done but am I prepared to risk major head trauma, broken ankle or worse?)

I could venture up to his office, lock the door behind me - obviously with him in there - and force him to listen. But what if he's not interested? Very public rejection is definitely up there in my top 10 ways to be humiliated.

And anyway, I don't think I've got the nerve to confront him without being fairly well oiled (I might have mentioned I'm not good with confrontation...)

Should I send him another text? What if he doesn't answer – what do I do then?

An email, what about an email? Then I think back to Dine Leavers and shudder.

Definitely not a good idea!

I've got just over a week to put my case forward before leave. My gut instinct tells me that once the holidays have begun, it'll be too late...

Week 14

Monday 7 December

O915 Getting ready for a meeting with Commander NTE (just can't get used to calling him Steve). He wants an update on our Internationals.

I already have a pretty good idea of who's likely to make the grade (and more importantly who's not) but I have to be a little bit cagey as my predictions could all go down the Swannee after the Speaking Tests are finished today...

And, for obvious reasons, I don't really want to be left with egg on my face (not to mention the fact that the RN have an irritating habit of throwing the 'You said...' back at you, with unfailing regularity - for pretty much, well, ever).

I'm actually thankful to have something to focus on other than my abysmal situation with the man who I suspect may well be the love of my life.

I've spent the whole weekend beating myself up to the frustration of my best friend, sibling and daughters In fact I actually thought Frankie was going to commit bodily violence on me at one point after I wailed "What am I going to dooooo?" for the 50th time.

Their collective advice was "Bloody well speak to him."

It's ok for them; they haven't seen him in grim, forbidding, not to mention downright scary mode. Of course, 'them' is actually confined to Frankie because she's the only one who's seen him at all (and Nelson of course – but he hasn't ventured an opinion as of yet.)

I've got 4 more days after today...

Tuesday 8 December

1 **500** We've got the final test results and it looks like we've got a whopping 80% pass rate – woo hoo.

I've emailed the results to the appropriate Embassies and the PTB and now getting ready to break the news to the remaining 20% that they're going to be with us for another term...

1700 Have informed the condemned 7 of their less than illustrious fate – although given that most of them were Qatar Coastguard, their primary concern seemed to be whether this meant they could go on leave early.

HRH took it very well – but not actually sure he completely understood...

A helicopter will be coming for him on Thursday after the Passing Out Parade has finished. In theory, we'll see him again in January...

Still haven't spoken to Rob.

Wednesday 9 December

1615 Still haven't spoken to Rob and now getting seriously panicky.

I actually took the bull by horns this afternoon and made my way up to his office (we had the Wardroom Christmas lunch so had a couple of glasses of wine – medicinal of course, resulting in some much needed dutch courage).

Unfortunately he wasn't there.

Now just left with a resounding headache.

Tomorrow's the Passing Out Parade, so there might not be any time to speak to him then and I don't know if he's going to the Christmas Ball on Friday.

I'm running out of time.

Think I'm going to have to resort to sending him a text...

2130 I'm sitting in the living room with Rosie, Frankie and James for a serious brainstorming session.

We (by that I mean they) have decided that the text should be short and to the point – requesting an opportunity for us both to talk privately (oh God I feel sick just thinking about it...)

However, it takes another couple of glasses of wine before I work up the courage to send it...

2200 No response...

2230 No response...

2300 No response.

2330 Still no response.

It's looking like another sleepless night.

Thursday 10 December

O730 Needless to say, I've been awake for most of the night; but, you know what? It seems that managing to count up to 5000 sheep can actually have a positive effect.

I really don't want this anymore. I'm knackered, miserable, fed-up, depressed and what's more, I've simply HAD ENOUGH! I WILL speak to him today – come hell or high water; and what's more, he WILL listen to what I have to say...

I have already decided what I'm going to wear (Passing Out Parades only take place once a term and they're always a good opportunity to dress up.)

I've settled on a black and red fitted dress (an old faithful but does flatter the curves) teamed with a red bolero jacket – festive as well as classy.

AND it's back to the red lips. Subtlety has gone out of the window. Subtlety has left the building...

I CAN DO THIS!

1000 Time to go down to the Wardroom. The Passing Out Parade (POP – of course) kicks off at 1030 and the guests have already started to arrive. Looking out of a classroom window, I can see a plethora of hats and 'faux' furs on the ramps around the Parade Ground (not raining so far but bloody cold).

I can see the Commander standing near the main entrance to the

College (wearing a bit more than the last time I saw him on the ramps).

The salute today is being taken by the supreme head of the Royal Navy – The First Sea Lord no less (I always think that's such a cracking title – First Sea Lord; brilliant.)

To be fair, it's not quite as exciting as having the salute taken by one of the Royals (of course we're very used to royalty gracing our Parade Ground - the RN being the senior service, don't you know...)

1015 The Wardroom is heaving. I look around for Rob, determined to corner him at the first opportunity.
I spot him over by the windows – bugger, it looks as if he's hosting a couple of VIPs which means I'm going to have to wait.

He glances over and catches me staring at him. For once, I don't look away, but simply stare back (aiming for challenging yet wistful - bloody difficult I can tell you).

He holds my gaze for a few seconds, then looks away with a slight frown.

That's good, got him thinking (I hope.)

1030 Everyone attending the POP has made their way out of the Wardroom and onto the Parade Ground leaving just a few of us who are fortunate enough to be able to watch the whole thing through the windows. I love the whole ambience of the POP; just prefer it in the summer...

And then we're off as the Royal Marine band begins marching onto the Parade Ground with a rousing chorus of Anchors Aweigh...

1200 Once the First Sea Lord (they call him 1SL...) has inspected every cadet (can take a while although they usually get a move on when everyone's standing around freezing their gonads off), it's time for the finale, as all the cadets march around the ramps saluting the Admiral as they pass. Once the salute has been taken, they briefly return to the Parade Ground before marching slowly up the steps and into the main entrance. The last bit as always is accompanied by the haunting strains of Auld Lang Syne which never fails to bring a lump to my throat.

Then it's over, signalled by a rousing cheer coming from the depths of The Corridor from all those who've just passed out (not literally, obviously – don't think we had any keel over during the ceremony; too bloody cold).

Right, I need to get on to the Quarterdeck quickly – this is where I have to do my bit along with John – meeting and greeting all the International guests during the drinks reception.

Although wine is available to all guests, John and I are unable to partake due to the fact that most of the guests we look after are Muslim – which on this occasion is not helping with my whole 'I can do this' mind-set. As I surreptitiously watch Rob across the room, I can feel my bravado slowly trickling away...

I look down at my watch – only 45 minutes until I can go for lunch. I take a deep breath; I'll collar him then (and have a backbone inducing glass of wine at the same time).

1350 Ok it's now or never. Most of the guests have departed, leaving officers and civilian staff to relax with relief now all the pomp and ceremony is over.

Rob is sitting in the bar with Sam and several others. They already have a good few empty bottles on the table in front of them as they begin the unwinding process at the end of a long term. (Officers in the RN do take their 'unwinding' very seriously – the procedure can last a full 24 hours once they've started...!)

I can see that Rob has gone as far as undoing his ceremonial jacket and is laughing at something Sam is saying.

Does that mean he's more or less likely to listen to what I have to say…?

Does he even care – oh God, he doesn't look like he does.

I'm sitting over the other side of the room with the language teachers. Our Internationals are busy packing their gear back in their cabins. Once they've reported back to the Language School, they'll be given permission to go on leave (always a bit hit and miss as to whether they'll miss out the 'permission to go' bit and simply do a runner).

To be honest, at this point in time, I'm too knackered and jaded to care.

They don't know how lucky they are…

The teachers begin to get up in preparation to see off their students. I tell them I'll be along in a minute to give my 'Head of English Language Training' end of term speech.

Under normal circumstances, I'd be quite emotional about seeing our prodigies move on into 'big school'.

Under normal circumstances.

1400 I've got about 5 minutes to do this. I was hoping that Rob might get up to go to the heads (alone) but no such luck.

My heart is pounding behind my rib cage and the chicken korma I had for lunch is sitting like a lump of lead in the pit of my stomach.

As I get up and walk towards potential, very public, humiliation, I reflect that this whole 'love' thing really stinks.

Rob has his back to me so doesn't see me coming – not so Sam unfortunately; he throws his arms in the air and shouts me over like we haven't seen each other for years (hope Rob's not quite as trollied).

My nemesis swivels round to face me and I hesitate a few feet away.

"Er Rob," My voice cracks so I cough and start again.
"I was wondering if you had time for a quick word." He frowns
(I've just realized he's actually pretty good at that) before saying
in a very uninterested voice, "Sure, go ahead"

"Erm, I'd like to do it privately if that's ok…" I just want the
ground to swallow me up.

For one horrific second I think he's going to refuse and I actually
begin backing away in preparation to flee the room.

Then he shrugs and gets out of his chair, waving me on to go first
to wherever I have in mind. There are a few sniggers behind us as
I lead the way into the Wardroom cloakroom.

Then all too soon we are standing staring at one another under
the dubious concealment of a couple of coats and caps.

"What is it?" His eyes are giving nothing away and his voice still
sounds frankly bored and, even worse, completely aloof.

I take a deep breath. "Did you get my text?"

He simply continues to look at me as he nods and I realise at that
moment that he really is not going to make this easy.

Fighting the temptation to turn and run, I rush on (I've
rehearsed this speech so many times, I have to make sure I get it
all out in a oner in case he tries to interrupt…)

"Look the thing is I think I made a mistake I assumed after
seeing her in your cabin that you and Tracy were still together
and thing is I'm so scared of being hurt again but I had such a
wonderful time when we were sailing and I really like you and I
was wondering if you'd consider you know giving it another go
seeing as we seemed to enjoy each other's company and seeing as
you're not actually you know with Tracy or at least I don't think
you are you said you hadn't seen her since Sunday which I think

means you're not with her so would you consider being with me I think I might have actually fallen in love with you..."

Rob blinks as I grind to a halt. I didn't mean to let the last bit slip...

My heart is racing and my hands are clenched so tightly that my nails are digging in to my palms.

After what seems like an eternity of silence (but was probably only a few seconds), he closes his eyes briefly and sighs. Then he steps towards me and without taking his eyes off mine, he simply raises his hand and lays his palm gently against my cheek.

His eyes are now warm and bright, bright blue.

"Will you go to the ball with me tomorrow night?"

Epilogue

Friday 11 December

1930 The whole College is decorated with festoons of holly and mistletoe. As we stand at the entrance to the Quarterdeck, I take in the beautiful garlands of fairy lights adorning the Poopdeck as well as the gigantic Christmas tree - all twinkling and reflecting the swathes of tinsel and hundreds of baubles that nestle within the beautiful green branches. The smell of pine needles permeates the room along with echoes of laughter and carefree banter.

I glance up at the man next to me who is gazing at me in appreciation. "You look absolutely stunning tonight," He murmurs, admiration so very evident in his voice.
And to be fair, I really do! My red satin ball gown fits me flawlessly and is totally perfect for the evening.

If there's one thing I'm good at – it's dressing for the occasion…

Rob holds out his arm and I slip my hand into it. "Shall we go in?" He asks.

"Absolutely," I say, and, as I smile up at him, my heart actually feels like it's going to burst with happiness

Think it's definitely a sign…

THE END

Author's Note

The beautiful yachting haven of Dartmouth in South Devon holds a very special place in my heart – not least because I met my husband there :-)

If you're ever in the area, please take the time out to visit. The pubs and restaurants I describe are real and I've spent many a happy lunchtime/evening in each of them

If you'd like more information about Dartmouth and the surrounding areas, here's a link to the Tourist Information Centre.

https://discoverdartmouth.com

~*~

And lastly, thanks a million for taking the time to read this story and on the next page I have included a sneak preview of *Claiming Victory*. For those of you who are interested, it's the first book in my series of romantic comedies entitled *The Dartmouth Diaries*

I really hope we can continue on to the next one together...

Yours aye (just had to get that in!)

Bev

Claiming Victory

Claiming Victory is a funny contemporary romantic comedy that will appeal to every woman who still believes fairy tales can come true...

..."So let me get this straight Admiral. Your plan is to somehow get the most famous actor in the world, to fall in love with your daughter Victory, who we both love dearly, but - and please don't take offence Sir - who you yourself admit is built generously across the aft, and whose face is unlikely to launch the Dartmouth ferry, let alone a thousand ships..."

Victory Shackleford is a spinster, or at least well on the way to becoming one. She is thirty two years old, still lives with her father - an eccentric retired Admiral, and the love of her life is a dog.

She thinks her father is reckless, irresponsible, and totally incapable of looking after himself. He thinks his daughter is a boring nagging harpy with no imagination or sense of adventure and what's more, he's determined to get her married off.

Unfortunately there's no one in the picturesque yachting town of Dartmouth that Tory is remotely interested in, despite her father's best efforts.

But all that is about to change when she discovers that her madcap father has rented out their house as a location shoot for the biggest blockbuster of the year. As cast and crew descend, Tory's humdrum orderly existence is turned completely upside down, especially as the lead actor has just been voted the sexiest man on the planet...

Book One in a new romance series and full of romantic humour, Claiming Victory is a must for fans of funny love stories, especially quirky British Romantic comedies.

Chapter One

Admiral Charles Shackleford (retired) entered the dimly lit interior of his favourite watering hole. Once inside he waited for a second for his eyes to adjust and glanced around to check that his aging springer spaniel was already seated beside his stool at the bar. Pickles had disappeared into the undergrowth half a mile back as they were walking along the wooded trail high above the picturesque River Dart after the scent of some poor unfortunate rabbit caught his still youthful nose. The Admiral was not unduly worried; this was a regular occurrence and Pickles knew his way to the Ship Inn better than his master.

Satisfied that all was as it should be for a Friday lunchtime, Admiral Shackleford waved to the other regulars and made his way to his customary seat at the bar where his long standing (and long suffering) friend Jimmy Noone was already halfway down his first pint.

"You're a bit late today Sir," observed Jimmy, after saluting his former commanding officer smartly.

Charles Shackleford grunted as he heaved his ample bottom onto the bar stool.

"Got bloody waylaid by that bossy daughter of mine." He sighed dramatically before taking a long draft of his pint of real ale, already poured and placed on the bar in front of him.

"Damn bee in her bonnet since she found out about my

relationship with Mabel Pomfrey. Of course, I told her to mind her own bloody business, but it has to be said that the cat's out of the bag and no mistake."

He stared gloomily down into his pint. "She said it cast aspersions on her poor mother's memory. But what she don't understand Jimmy, is that I'm still a man in my prime. I've got needs. I mean look at me – why can't she see that I'm still a fine figure of a man and any woman would be more than happy to shack up with me."

Abruptly the Admiral turned towards his friend so that the light shone directly onto his face and leaned forward.

"Come on then man, tell me you agree."

Jimmy took a deep breath as he dubiously regarded the watery eyes, thread veined cheeks and larger than average nose no more than six inches in front of him.

However, before he could come up with a suitably acceptable reply that wouldn't result in him standing to attention for the next four hours in front of the Admiral's dishwasher, the latter turned away, either indicating that it was purely a rhetorical question or that he genuinely couldn't comprehend that anyone could possibly regard him as less than a prime catch.

Jimmy sighed with relief. He really hadn't got time this afternoon to do dishwasher duty as he'd agreed to take his wife shopping. Although to be fair, a four hour stint in front of an electrical appliance at the Admiral's house with Tory sneaking him tea and biscuits was actually preferable to four hours trailing after his wife in Marks and Spencer's. He didn't think his wife would see it that way though. Emily Noone had enough trouble understanding her husband's tolerance towards 'that dinosaur's' eccentricities as it was.

276

Of course, Emily wasn't aware that only the quick thinking of the dinosaur in question had, early on in their naval career, saved her husband from a potentially horrible fate involving a Thai prostitute who'd actually turned out to be a man...

As far as Jimmy was concerned, Admiral Shackleford was his Commanding Officer and always would be and if that involved such idiosyncrasies as presenting himself in front of a dishwasher with headphones on, saluting and saying, "Dishwasher manned and ready sir," and then four hours later, saluting again while saying, "Dishwasher secured," then so be it.

It was a small price to pay...

He leaned towards his morose friend and patted him on the back, showing a little manly support (acceptable, even from subordinates), while murmuring, "Don't worry about it too much Sir. Tory's a sensible girl. She'll come round eventually – you know she wants you to be happy." The Admiral's only response was an inelegant snort, so Jimmy ceased his patting and went back to his pint.

Both men gazed into their drinks for a few minutes as if all the answers would be found in the amber depths.

"What she needs is a man." Jimmy's abrupt observation drew another rude snort, this one even louder.

"Who do you suggest? She's not interested in anyone. Says there's no one in Dartmouth she'd give house room to and believe me I've tried. When she's not giving me grief, she spends all her time in that bloody gallery with all them airy fairy types. Can't imagine any one of them climbing her rigging. Not one set of balls between 'em."

Jimmy chuckled at the Admiral's description of Tory's testosterone challenged male friends.

"She's not ugly though," Charles Shackleford mused, still staring into his drink. "She might have an arse the size of an aircraft carrier, but she's got her mother's top half which balances it out nicely."

"Aye, she's built a bit broad across the beam," Jimmy agreed nodding his head.

"And then there's this bloody film crew. I haven't told her yet." Jimmy frowned at the abrupt change of subject and raising his head, shot a puzzled glance over to the Admiral.

"Film crew? What film crew?"

Charles Shackleford looked back irritably. "Come on Jimmy, get a grip. I'm talking about that group of nancies coming to film at the house next month. I must have mentioned it.

Jimmy simply shook his head in bewilderment.

Frowning at his friend's obtuseness, the Admiral went on, "You know, what's that bloody film they're making at the moment – big blockbuster everyone's talking about?"

"What, you mean 'The Bridegroom?"

"That's the one. Seems like they were looking for a large house overlooking the River Dart. Needed the mooring too. Think they were hoping for Greenway, you know, Agatha Christie's place, but then they spied 'The Admiralty' and said it was spot on. Paying me a packet they are. Coming next week"

Jimmy stared at his former commanding officer with something approaching pity. "And you've arranged all this without telling Tory?"

"None of her bloody business," The Admiral blustered, banging his now empty pint glass on the bar and waving at the bar maid for a refill. "She's out most of the time anyway."

Jimmy shook his head in disbelief. "When are you going to tell her?"

"Was going to do it this morning, but then this business with Mabel came up so I scarpered. Last I saw she was taking that bloody little mongrel of hers out for a walk. Hoping she'll walk off her temper." This last was said in a tone of voice that indicated that in the Admiral's opinion, there was more likelihood of hell freezing over.

"Is Noah Westbrook coming?" said Jimmy, suddenly sensing a bit of gossip he could pass on to Emily.

"Noah who?" was the Admiral's bewildered response.

"Noah Westbrook. Come on Sir, you must know him. He's the most famous actor in the world. Women go completely gaga over him. If nothing else, that should make Tory happy."

The Admiral stared at him thoughtfully. "What's he look like, this Noah West..chappy?"

The bar maid, who had been unashamedly listening to the whole conversation, couldn't contain herself any longer and, thrusting a glossy magazine under the Admiral's nose, said breathlessly, "Like this. He looks like this."

The full colour photograph was that of a naked man lounging on a sofa, with only a towel protecting his modesty, together with the caption 'Noah Westbrook, officially voted the sexiest man on the planet.'

Admiral Charles Shackleford stared pensively down at the picture in front of him. "So this Noah chap – he's in this film is he?"

"He's got the lead role." The bar maid actually twittered causing the Admiral to look up in irritation – bloody woman must 50 if she's a day. Shooting her a withering look, he went back to the magazine and read the beginning of the article inside.

"Noah Westbrook is to be filming in the South West of England over the next month causing a sudden flurry of bookings to hotels and guest houses in the South Devon area".

The Admiral continued to stare at the photo, the germination of an idea tiptoeing around the edges of his brain.

Glancing up, he discovered that he was the subject of scrutiny from not just the bar maid but by now the whole pub were waiting with bated breath to hear what he was going to say next.

The Admiral's eyes narrowed as the beginnings of a plan slowly began taking shape. But he needed to keep it under wraps. Looking around at his rapt audience, he feigned nonchalance. "Don't think Noah Westbrook was mentioned at all in the correspondence; think he must be filming somewhere else."

Then, without saying anything further, he downed the rest of his drink and climbed laboriously off his stool.

"Coming Jimmy, Pickles?" His tone was deceptively casual which fooled Jimmy not at all and, sensing something momentous afoot, the smaller man swiftly finished his pint and in his haste to follow the Admiral out of the door, only narrowly avoided falling over Pickles who, completely unappreciative of the need for urgency, was sitting in the middle of the floor, unconcernedly scratching behind his ear.

Once outside, the Admiral didn't bother waiting for his dog, secure in the knowledge that someone would let the disobedient hound out before he got too far down the road. Instead he took hold of Jimmy's arm and dragged him out of earshot – just in case anyone was listening.

In complete contrast to his mood on arrival, Charles Shackleford was now grinning from ear to ear. "That's it; I've finally got a plan," he hissed to his bewildered friend. "I'm going to get her married off."

"Who to?" asked Jimmy confused.

"Don't be so bloody slow Jimmy. To him of course. The actor chappy, Noah Westbrook. According to that magazine, women everywhere fall over themselves for him. Even Victory won't be able to resist him."

Jimmy opened his mouth but nothing came out. He stared in complete disbelief as the Admiral went on. "Then she'll move out and Mabel can move in. Simple."

Pickles came ambling up as Jimmy finally found his voice.

"So, let me get this straight Sir. Your plan is to somehow get Noah Westbrook, the most famous actor on the entire planet to fall in love with your daughter Victory, who we both love dearly, but - and please don't take offence Sir - who you yourself admit is built generous across the aft and whose face is unlikely to launch the Dartmouth ferry let alone a thousand ships."

The Admiral frowned. "Well admittedly, I've not worked out the finer details, but that's about the sum of it.

"What do you think...?"

The Dartmouth Diaries:

Claiming Victory: Book One
Sweet Victory: Book Two

All For Victory: Book Three
Chasing Victory: Book Four
Lasting Victory: Book Five
A Shackleford Victory: Book Six
Final Victory to be released on 13th December 2024

Keeping in Touch

Thank you so much for reading *An Officer and a Gentleman Wanted,* I really hope you enjoyed it.

For any of you who'd like to connect, I'd really love to hear from you. Feel free to contact me via my facebook page: https://www.facebook.com/beverleywattsromanticcomedyauthor or my website: http://www.beverleywatts.com

If you'd like me to let you know as soon as my next book is available, sign up to my newsletter by copying and pasting the link below into your browser and I'll keep you updated about all my latest releases.

https://motivated-teacher-3299.ck.page/143a008c18

Turn the page for a full list of my books available on Amazon.

Books Available on Amazon

The Dartmouth Diaries:

Book 1 - Claiming Victory
Book 2 - Sweet Victory
Book 3 - All for Victory
Book 4 - Chasing Victory
Book 5 - Lasting Victory
Book 6 - A Shackleford Victory
Book 7 - Final Victory to be released on 13th December 2024

The Admiral Shackleford Mysteries

Book 1 - A Murderous Valentine
Book 2 - A Murderous Marriage
Book 3 - A Murderous Season

The Shackleford Sisters

Book 1 - Grace
Book 2 - Temperance
Book 3 - Faith
Book 4 - Hope
Book 5 - Patience
Book 6 - Charity
Book 7 - Chastity
Book 8 - Prudence
Book 9 - Anthony

The Shackleford Legacies

Book 1 - Jennifer to be released on 20th June 2024

About The Author

Beverley Watts

Beverley spent 8 years teaching English as a Foreign Language to International Military Students in Britannia Royal Naval College, the Royal Navy's premier officer training establishment in the UK. She says that in the whole 8 years there was never a dull moment and many of her wonderful experiences at the College were not only memorable but were most definitely 'the stuff of fiction.' Her debut novel An Officer And A Gentleman Wanted is very loosely based on her adventures at the College.

Beverley particularly enjoys writing books that make people laugh and currently she has two series of Romantic Comedies, both contemporary and historical, as well as a humorous cosy mystery series under her belt.

She lives with her husband in an apartment overlooking the sea on the beautiful English Riviera. Between them they have 3 adult children and two gorgeous grandchildren plus a menagerie of animals including 5 dogs - 3 Romanian rescues of indeterminate breed called Florence, Trixie, and Lizzie, a neurotic 'Chorkie' named Pepé and a 'Chichon" named Dotty who was the inspiration for Dotty in The Dartmouth Diaries.

You can find out more about Beverley's books at www.beverleywatts.com

Printed in Great Britain
by Amazon

46033560R00165